DEAD AND DYING
ANGELS

VOLUME ONE
OF THE DOS CRUCES TRILOGY

DEAD AND DYING
ANGELS

by

JAMES A. MANGUM

JOHN M. HARDY PUBLISHING
ALPINE & HOUSTON

2005

First Printing: January 2005

1 3 5 7 9 8 6 4 2

ISBN 0-9717667-2-X

Printed and Bound in the United States of America

Jacket design — Leisha Israel, Blue Sky Media
Austin, Texas

John M. Hardy Publishing Company
Houston, Texas

www.johnmhardy.com

To the miracles in my life:
Jeremy, Jamie, Jill, Jodie, Taylor . . . and Connie.

"Real tragedy is never resolved.
It goes on hopelessly forever."

—Chinua Achebe

CONTENTS

PART III
Redemption, Resurrection, and Reparation

DEAD AND DYING
ANGELS

PART I

Please Excuse Me, I'm Killing Myself

Chapter 1

God and I Make a Deal

God and I have this deal. We got together on it forty-six years ago. I remember it well. It was my birthday, November 29, 1957. I'm sitting here *en mi casa pequeña* in Dos Cruces, Texas, on an old couch so ugly that the *viejo* who picks up junk wouldn't touch it. It's kind of a chartreuse color, although I suspect it's taken many years to achieve this shade of green. And of course you can see the springs and the cotton stuffing, now a sickly grayish, brain matter color, but who would have thought the old man wouldn't even haul it off. It doesn't matter much now.

I happen to be looking at this one-eyed dog, part blue heeler and the rest Dos Cruces hybrid, or should I say he's looking at me — not exactly with contempt, closer to subtle sarcasm. Like, "I knew you were the kind to do something like this, why should I be surprised?" But then again, I might just be projecting.

You see, I happen to be holding a Model 59 Smith

& Wesson between my teeth. One thing you should know about killing yourself: if you're going to do it, do it fast. Not only do you start having second thoughts — especially with a one-eyed, judgmental, wonder dog watching — but your jaws get tired. And inside my head, a voice keeps saying, "What's wrong with this picture?" It's my voice, but it's God talking.

Here's what I asked God to do when I was nine years old. "Whenever I do something bad, as in a sin, please punish me here on earth, because if Hell is any worse than this, I couldn't take it." That was the deal. It's an ironclad, non-negotiable, no loopholes contract. That was my idea. I told Him, "Even if I beg to be let out of this deal, anytime during my life, don't do it." I knew then, at only nine years old, that there would be many times I would try to renege on this agreement. And, oh how right I was. But there's one thing I can say about God: He keeps His word.

Chapter 2

Dos Cruces, Texas

Before I tell you about what happened on November 29, 1957, I want to tell you a little about Dos Cruces, Texas. Dos Cruces is different. It's hard to explain without your thinking I'm just making it up. It's like something out of the 30s and 40s, maybe the 1830s and 40s. In its heyday, which was very short-lived, Dos Cruces was an onion-growing mecca. Then came the Great Depression, and the town withered. The old red brick general store, Dos Cruces Mercantile, was closed for good in the 1970s. Now it's boarded up and falling down. There's a mom-and-pop grocery store, three cafe/beer joints, four gas stations, and a Post Office. The population is ninety-nine percent Hispanic and one hundred percent quirky.

The main road through town is Highway 199. It's also the only paved road in Dos Cruces. Beside it runs the Union Pacific tracks. Dos Cruces is the only place I've ever known where both sides of the tracks are on the wrong side of town.

Interestingly enough, the Southern Pacific Railroad Company originally surveyed the town around the turn of the century, and then apparently surveyed it again. The surveys don't match, which is no big deal until you try to buy or sell a piece of property in Dos Cruces. This is a rare occurrence, since no one in his or her right mind would want to buy a place here. Except for my dad, which is how I found out about the survey problem.

Surprisingly, nobody seems to want to sell either. Maybe they know that it would be a true effort in futility. Basically, all of the lots in town, according to one of the railroad surveys, overlap adjacent lots on the north side by approximately 10 feet. So everyone here is joined at the plot.

As a big shot in the oil and gas "bidness" once told me, Dos Cruces is about forty miles from Laredo and forty light years from anywhere else. And it's one of the hottest, driest places on earth. The dirt roads (redundant, since all roads are dirt around here) are reddish brown in color. The red dust permeates. It is omnipresent. Dos Cruces is located in the heart of what's known as "brush country." This means there are no large trees, except in town, and those are mostly salt cedars.

Salt cedars epitomize this country. They are ornery and kind of ugly to look at. They constantly drop their needle-like leaves, which, because of the high saline content, kill everything around them except the tree itself. Probably some kind of defense mechanism. Or maybe another one of God's sick nature jokes. And I guess I have a certain twisted admiration for their ability to survive in such a harsh place. The same can be said of the people here. And no, the analogy of one living thing inadvertently killing everything around it has not escaped me.

The brush country itself is an optical illusion. It looks flat and treeless. However, upon closer inspection, assuming you stick around long enough to inspect, you will see that it's a virtual forest, albeit a dwarfish one. You can't see the scrubby forest for the scrubby trees.

In the undulating outback the mesquite trees are not particularly impressive, but they are still trees, some fifteen or twenty feet tall. The *guajillo*, or whitebrush, grows beneath the mesquite. There is blackbrush, *huisache*, prickly pear, and buffelgrass persisting under the *guajillo*. Tough plant life for a tough environment.

The wildlife food chain includes javelinas, coyotes, roadrunners, various hawks and other raptors, whitetail deer, jackrabbits, rattlesnakes, scorpions, and ants. Tough animal life for a tough environment. It seems like everything in these parts has thorns, horns, claws, or stingers. And the world around Dos Cruces seems to be coated with red-brown dust. Even the people. Maybe even their souls. At least most of them.

Did I mention that I am the only real gringo — not counting the crazy people, the other crazy people that is — among the permanent residents of five hundred or so in Dos Cruces? By that I mean, the only person who doesn't speak Spanish, even Tex-Mex, well. Sure there are a few Anglos here, but they're fluent, especially in Tex-Mex.

There are a couple of exceptions: the old German couple, *los alemanes*, who arrived in the 1940s, shortly after World War II. I think you get the picture. People think they are Nazi war criminals. They don't talk to anyone, so they could be multi-lingual as far as anybody knows. They're none too friendly, but they do keep their tiny white frame house and little white picket fence freshly painted. You might say obsessively painted. When you walk or drive by their house you receive the look of death.

Another interesting fact about Dos Cruces is that nobody allows grass to grow in their yard. I'm the only exception. As a matter of fact, that's how I met Daniel. His Dos Cruces name is Borrego, but he is also called Goatboy. He came to mow my yard — it had gone native, it was a jungle. The ubiquitous buffelgrass had grown into vast clumps of lawn mower assassins. Dandelions and other tall nasty weeds were patient spectators, waiting, hoping for the mechanical carnage to begin. I told Daniel to be careful, there could be javelinas in there. He laughed. But then again, he laughs at everything. You see, laughter is Daniel, the goatboy's, totally useless defense mechanism. Everyone else's yard is red-brown dirt. Even the suspected Nazi couple has adopted this custom. The natives get out their grubbing hoes whenever a blade of grass has the audacity to show up in their yard. Daniel's family, in particular, embraced the ritual killing of vegetation. Once, driving by their collection of shanties, I saw Daniel and five or six family members with hoes, scythes and other homemade instruments of botanical death participating in an orgy of chlorophyll-letting.

I understand quite a bit of Spanish, mostly Tex-Mex, and can speak a little, but only when I have to. In a way, I wish I didn't understand any. *Yo no comprendo* — I wish. If I had not understood, then I might not be sitting here right now, eating an S&W sandwich.

Dos Cruces is the loneliest place on earth. Even to someone who is used to being alone. There are some really good people in Dos Cruces. And now there are three fewer evil ones.

Señor Zaragosa (*el viejo que habla con los muertos* ... the old man who talks with the dead) died last night. I had been sitting with him thirteen hours straight. Before he died though, he spoke to me in Spanish. "*Hablé con blanca bonita, Josefina. Voy con ella y Consuela y Julia.*" (I talked to pretty white Josie. I'm going with her, Connie, and Julie.) That's right. He said he talked with my daughter Josie last night. He said he's going to meet her, my other daughter Julie, and my wife Connie. Of course this is impossible. They were killed in a car wreck in Houston three years ago. You see, I sealed their fate when I was nine years old and made the deal with God.

I killed three men in Dos Cruces, Texas, and I'm working on the fourth. Myself. I don't want to talk about the killings just yet. But I will say, and I think you will agree, once you've heard the whole story, that they deserved it. I guess it's fair to conclude that you will be the jury of my peers by which I will be judged. Not that it matters. Remember, God and I have a deal.

Chapter 3

I Was Born

I was born in the small South Texas town of Beckville on November 29, 1948. I know you don't care and neither do I, really. But I feel compelled to go over all of this, my life that is. And I will say this: it is an interesting, although extremely depressing story. You have probably detected a cynical, acerbic edge to my thought processes. It's due to the fact that I'm not sure you are real. Any of you.

I'm pretty sure that I'm real. So most of the time I feel like I'm just talking to myself. But if you are real, the story you are about to hear is just plain tragic — in so many ways. It's not really intended to be a cautionary tale. I've never been the type to preach to others. But there are lessons to be learned. And they are too late to be learned by me.

At birth, my mother forgot about me. It really wasn't her fault, I guess. She was crazy, and in 1948 there wasn't much anybody could do about it. So for the first nine months of my life here on earth, my Aunt Maggie raised me.

Aunt Maggie wasn't really a bad person. Cold maybe. She had two small children of her own, my cousins Wanda and Wilson. Wanda was four and Wilson was three, and I was a burden. Aunt Maggie didn't really need another fish to fry, so to speak. My two older brothers, Charles and Robert, lived with Aunt Bobbie, the nice aunt, for those nine months. At that time, Charlie was four years old and Bobby was two. My father and my hero, also named Charles, had his hands full working three jobs. He was trying to make those proverbial ends meet. It cost a lot to have your wife go crazy in 1948. And not just in money.

So when I was nine months old, my two brothers, my mom, my dad and I all moved into a little, white, asbestos-shingled house in the country two miles from Mineral, Texas. Two miles from nowhere.

Chapter 4

All the Caliche Dust You Could Eat

My father's main job was working for Gas Products, Inc., a small oil and gas company. He was a pumper, sometimes called a gauger. That's the guy that takes care of the oil and gas wells. It's pretty much the bottom of the food chain in the "oil bidness," as we call it here in Texas. The little white house, known as a "lease house," was owned by the company. It was situated on their thousand-plus-acre oil and gas lease. It wasn't a bad place to grow up, basically a thousand acre back yard, but the sulfur water the well pumped smelled and tasted like rotten eggs.

Mesquite and oak trees dotted the rolling landscape and the Maxwell family had all the caliche dust we could eat. Caliche. It's the first word that interested me as a child. I still like to say it every chance I get. Ka-lee-chay. It's a layer of soil held together by calcium carbonate. It's white. It's used to pave roads on oil and gas leases. It's so South Texas. I remember seeing my dad driving his beat-up pickup down the lease roads, caliche dust roiling in his wake. To me it was always a happy sight.

South Texas is hot as Hell in the summer. Summers last from April to September, so when I say it was hot, I mean it was hot for a long time. And poor oilfield trash didn't have air conditioning. Back then only a few rich people did. I sometimes think maybe the heat and isolation drove my mother crazy, but I know better. She was born depressed, just like I was. Eventually the depression drives you crazy. At least that's the way it was in 1948. Now, they have some new and really amazing drugs for depression. I can attest to that.

Charles, my dad, also looked after some oil wells on the side for another little company. And in his "spare time," he worked at the only gas station in Mineral. He was the hardest working person I have ever known — and the kindest. But since he worked so hard, I didn't get to see him much. I'm not saying my father didn't get mad, he got mad at us boys plenty of times. He would yell and stomp around for about 15 seconds. I think that was his mad limit. But he never got mad at my mother. True love, like God, works in mysterious ways (although God isn't all that mysterious once you get to know Him). When I was older I realized my dad got mad at my brothers and me mostly out of the frustration of living with my mother. But even when I was a little boy, I always forgave him. I now know that he worked all of the time, not just for the money, but to stay away from his crazy wife. True love is also contradictory.

Chapter 5

Bouncing and Catching

The first nine years of my life were pretty uneventful, and, with a couple of exceptions, I really don't remember much of it. My mother slept most of the time. I found out later it was because when she wasn't sleeping, she was drinking — and vice versa. For those nine years, I only remember two incidents that involved my mother and me.

First, bathing with her when I was about three years old I remember how hairy she was "down there." You're going to laugh, but up until that time in my life the only thing that had ever really frightened me was tarantulas. Two or three times a year one would show up in the yard, so I thought one had shown up in the bathtub on my mom. I was too intimidated to say anything, but I moved as far away as possible in the tub. It scared the hell out of me, but I wasn't totally surprised. I know that sounds weird, but with my mother, anything was possible.

I also remember once making so much noise with my brothers that we woke her up. She chased us out of the house with a belt, using the buckle end as a weapon. She was crying and screaming. I was probably five years old then. We hid under the house and waited for her to go back into hibernation.

The other things I remember about those nine years are:

Running away from home when I was about four years old. My dad caught me about a half-mile down a caliche lease road and whipped my little butt all the way home.

Climbing up and on top of a 20-foot-high oil storage tank when I was four or five years old and my father slowly walking up the steel ladder talking very calmly to me. At the top of the ladder was a landing with an angle-iron handrail. I was hanging onto the handrail looking down at the ground. He grabbed me before I could fall. I remember the story so clearly because my dad told it many times over the years. He would have a trace of fear in his voice when he told it.

When I was six, cutting my hand on a coffee can lid. It was my right hand — my throwing hand. My parents didn't take me to the doctor. They probably couldn't afford it. I closed my hand and wouldn't open it for three or four months — probably torn tendons and ligaments. My dad and my brothers claim that I finally opened it when my Uncle Beason, Maggie's husband, offered me some pocket change. I don't remember that part of the story, but this injury did allow me to become somewhat ambidextrous.

Having an asthma attack the only time my parents

ever threw a party. I remember Chinese lanterns outside and how pretty they looked and how bad I felt. I remember a lot of people talking and laughing and the smell of barbeque. I had developed asthma, not helped by the fact that both of my parents smoked like furnaces. I guess I was seven or eight years old then. I thought I was going to quit breathing.

But what I remember most about living out on that oil and gas lease was the constant and exquisite loneliness.

I see myself bouncing a rubber ball off the concrete backdoor steps; a little boy wearing nothing but underwear, bouncing and catching, bouncing and catching. My father was working, my mother was sleeping, and my brothers were off exploring our thousand-acre back yard. As I got older, I would throw the ball on the roof and catch it when it came down, pretending to be Duke Snider, the great Brooklyn Dodgers center fielder. After each catch I could hear the roar of the Ebbet's Field crowd. Oh, what a hero I was!

I would look out the back door of the lease house at night, watching the incredibly bright fires — actually flares to burn off natural gas coming out of the oil wells. They were intended to keep the gas from building up and causing an explosion. I would shiver in fear and awe, intuitively knowing that this was a message from God. But I couldn't figure out what it meant.

In this supernaturally lit night sky, up on a hill almost a half of a mile away, I could see the Mineral cemetery. In the eerie orange-yellow glow, the silhouettes of the two largest monuments, stone angels, side-by-side, seemed to be hovering just above the ground. Looking back with the perspective of fifty years of life on this earth, the two stone angels seemed to be drifting through Hell.

I don't really know if these things I remember have any particular relevance to my story, but they might. And since I'm telling this story mostly because I don't have a choice, that is to say God is making me, it doesn't make a whole lot of difference if they do or they don't.

Chapter 6

The Weak One Cut from the Herd

Before I confide in you about the thing that happened in 1957, there are some other particulars I need to cover. Memories, oozing from my mind like an old, festering wound. Not chronological, much like your memories, I suspect. Because we store them haphazardly, we stumble upon them at the oddest times and in the oddest places. Please bear with me for a while, I must talk about them in the third person.

What I am now is a result of my actions and my "covenant" with God. As a child I was often sick, and as a result, small for my age. I was a loner by destiny and maybe by choice. When I look back on the little boy I was, it's like looking at an old home movie with faded color, muted pastels, and no sound.

He is small and thin with light brown hair and a serious expression on his face — a cute kid, content just sitting on that sidewalk, bouncing the ball once before it rebounds off the steps back into his hands.

When he turns five, his mother arranges for him to attend Catholic school in Beckville with his two brothers. Public schools would not take him that young, but his mother needed him out of the house.

Until he started school, he was alone. Except for the memories of the belt and the tarantula thing, he didn't remember not feeling safe. Loneliness was not a concept to him, it was the way he lived. He was a solitary being and that was fine with him.

Then, when he entered the first grade at Saint Joseph's Catholic School, his life changed. He had been to church a few times, but really didn't remember it. It was as if he were in jail and had been taken out of solitary confinement and put in with the general population.

Now the 8mm movie morphs into a National Geographic Special, and a pack of hyenas cut the young, weak antelope out of the herd. Little Jamey Maxwell's one defense mechanism, his smile, happens to be totally useless.

On the first day of school he was beaten up by the third grade bully — just for being there. When Hubert, the bully, approached him, Jamey smiled. Big mistake, a sign of weakness. Charlie and Bobby were no help. They were busy defending themselves from other young thugs somewhere else on the playground. But at least they had each other.

When Charlie and Bobby found out about the beating Jamey had taken, they cleaned his bloody nose and took him to the water fountain for a drink. But things got worse.

Jamey was able to stay to himself during recess —

usually hiding in the shrubs around the rock church — but in the classroom, there was nowhere to hide.

Unless he was asked, he never said anything to anyone, particularly his teacher, Sister Margaret. And for some reason, she would ask and ask often. She had singled him out of the herd and he never seemed to have the right answer. His punishment was one of two things: the blackboard pointer across the butt, or Sister Margaret's knuckles hard to the head. It was always her choice. He preferred the pointer.

Somehow he was able to survive two additional playground beatings and the daily dose from Sister Margaret with only limited brain damage. Now he was old enough to attend public school.

Chapter 7

Short-Lived Respite

Public school wasn't bad. In the second and third grades, I went to a tiny school in Tulseta, about ten miles from Mineral. There were eight kids in my class, including me. I made friends mostly from riding the bus. My shy smile/their shy smile. It worked. Everyone called me little Jamey.

My brothers also fared well at Tulseta. Dad was working long hours, but he cooked supper for us at night, breakfast in the morning, and usually a sack lunch for school. My mother was still in hibernation, which was good news, I guess, for all of us. All was well at the Maxwell household. Had I been older, I might have known it wouldn't last.

Chapter 8

The Kind That Would Smile, Then Shoot You

Allow me, if you will (or if you won't), to jump ahead a bit. For twenty-five years I served as a Special Agent with the United States Customs Service in Houston. For a year before that, right out of college, I was a sky marshal. I flew on commercial airlines to prevent planes from being hijacked. I was an English major at Texas A&I University and couldn't find a job. Sky marshal was the first offer I got, so I took it. I had never handled a handgun and had never flown on an airplane. Four weeks later I was doing both. The year was 1971. I was twenty-two years old, still desperately shy, but now responsible for the lives of two hundred passengers and the crew — at 30,000 feet! The irony in this was manifest.

The Sky Marshal Program — jointly operated by the Federal Aviation Administration and the U.S. Customs Service — was Richard Nixon's idea. A really bad idea in my opinion. It lasted a couple of years and then someone invented metal detectors. Keep everybody with guns off the plane, including the sky marshals. A really good idea in my opinion. When the program folded, my ex-supervisor, who had gone on to become a Customs Special Agent, helped me get on there. That man liked me. He once told someone, "Watch that Jamey. He may be a quiet kid, but he's also the kind that would smile while pumping six rounds into you." At the time I wondered what the hell he was talking about. Now I know.

I felt compelled to prove that I was a real man. Or at least my idea of one. When we went on drug raids, I was always first through the door. When we arrested the bad guys, I always came on strong. The other guys, who were all older than me, saw me as mild-mannered and low-keyed at the office. So they were always amused watching me when we were kicking ass and taking names. I got a reputation for being the quiet, skinny kid (6 feet tall by then, but only 150 pounds) who would just as soon shoot you as look at you. They started calling me Clark Kent. They had no idea that I was mostly just scared that I wouldn't be man enough when the time came.

Chapter 9

Angels Walk the Earth in Dos Cruces

Angels walk the earth in Dos Cruces. I've seen them. One for sure. Her name is Violet. She doesn't speak. Her sister — at least people here say it's her sister — leads her around town by the hand. The natives just refer to both of them as *las hermanas*, the sisters.

They live with an old, one-armed man, about three Dos Cruces blocks down the dirt road from me, in a tiny adobe shack. Half the roof is gone. There is a wooden gate out front of the little shack. The gate is precariously hanging by one hinge, but it is closed. The funny thing is, aside from the two round posts holding the gate up, there is nothing left of the fence, if there ever was one. There is a crudely lettered, almost illegible, hand-painted sign on the gate. The sign says "SAEK TAU GOKU." Who knows what that means? Apparently no one. At least that's what I thought when I first saw the sign. As it turns out, it meant quite a lot. Three men, *Los Diablos*, died because of it.

The old man's last name is Dochler. No one knows his first name. Names aren't a big thing here in Dos Cruces — except for nicknames. He has only one arm. I should also say he has only one shoulder. In fact, he looks like he was cut in half by the tail rotor on a helicopter. It's hard to believe a man can live with so little left of his upper torso. Dochler looks to be about ninety years old. Getting cut in half may do that to you. They say he moved into town many years ago after he was let go from working on some ranch around here. No one seems to know which ranch or how long ago. Time and details aren't a big thing here in Dos Cruces either. They say the sisters just showed up in Dos Cruces one day, living with Dochler, known in Dos Cruces as half-man, *hombre medio*. No one knows their last names. What a surprise. Dos Cruces denizens don't really pay a lot of attention to *los locos*, the crazy ones. Maybe because everyone here is crazy. I know I am. You know the sign that says, "You don't have to be crazy to work here, but it sure helps." Well, if Dos Cruces had a city limit sign (it's not really a city since it's never been incorporated) it would read: "You don't have to be crazy to live here, but it sure helps. Angels also welcome."

Before I tell you how I know Violet is an angel, let me share a couple of observations I've made since I took up residence here three years ago. Crazy people — with a few exceptions — don't socialize with other crazy people. They are totally isolated. Alone in their own little world. It's almost as if they jealously guard their own insanity. When two crazy people's orbits collide, something or someone has to give. Violet and her sister would be considered crazy by any so-called rational person from the outside world. It's hard to guess Violet's age. It could be anywhere between forty-five and seventy. Her sister looks much older. But Violet is not crazy. That's why they can coexist. She's an angel, as I've told you. I know because God told me. I would have figured it out anyway.

When I say God tells me things, it's not that I hear His voice — or any other voices for that matter. I suffer from depression, not schizophrenia. It's just that He makes it clear to me. In my head. A sudden revelation or epiphany (I've always liked that word). Most things I have to figure out on my own. I realize that I'm rambling and I'm sure I'm being redundant and repetitive (ha, ha), but I have been up seventy-two hours straight. Also, I've consumed several (let's say eighteen or so) beers. And I am in the middle of committing suicide. So please forgive me.

The reason I know Violet's name is Violet is this: when her sister leads her around town by the hand, she yells her name. Repeatedly. The old crone says things like, "Goddamn it Violet, I told you we were gonna be late. That son-of-a-bitch on the goddamn bus is gonna run off and leave us, Violet. Goddamn son-of-a-bitch." I've witnessed this scene many times in my three years here in God's little paradise. And although it appears the old hag cusses a lot, she really only uses goddamn and son-of-a-bitch. But she uses them in all their possible combinations.

I've never actually seen the sisters get on the bus

(Greyhound stops here once a day, but I'm not sure why. No one ever gets on or gets off). And I've been told that in the many years they have lived here, no one has ever seen them get on the bus.

The other thing about Violet and her sister is something that is fairly common among crazy people (again, Violet's not crazy, but her sister is, and she, no doubt, dresses Violet). Even in the heat of the summer in Dos Cruces, where temperatures climb to 110 degrees on just about a daily basis, they always wear overcoats. They also wear knee length rubber boots. And they walk. A lot. I have seen them four or five miles from Dos Cruces, in the dead of night, stumbling and gliding along the highway, Miss Obscenity dragging Violet behind her.

But here is the amazing thing about Violet. She always looks appropriately dressed. Regal actually. Violet is beautiful. You might not think so at first. But if you watch her — like I have for three years — you see it. Her skin is as smooth and white as alabaster. No wrinkles, but you can tell she's been on Earth for a while. She looks timeless. Her eyes appear to be violet ("you're turning violet, Violet" — Willy Wonka, my Josie's favorite movie). Her hair is a thick mane of gray with white streaks — shoulder length. It doesn't really look like it's been combed, but it looks right. Do you know what I mean?

She is tall and thin and she walks erect. Like royalty. And even though her sister is always in a hurry — practically running, dragging Violet behind — Violet looks like she is slowly floating. Just off the ground. The look of serenity and aloofness on her face is the real giveaway to the fact she is actually an angel. Look closely. She does not reside here in Dos Cruces or even on this planet. Her head is perpetually pointed skyward at a 45-degree angle, eyes focused on some point in the universe far, far away. She wears a faint smile of ecstasy on her face. She looks beatific (I like this word too). Violet is not of this realm.

Her sister is at the opposite end of the existence spectrum. She is of the earth. She is of Dos Cruces. She is stoop-shouldered and short. Her face has white blotches all over it — some kind of skin disease. She is wiry with wiry white hair. Thorns, horns, claws, and stingers. She is loud. Her eyes are always on the red-brown dirt. She is always in a hurry. She is anything but regal.

Have you ever tried to smile with a Smith and Wesson Model 59 in your mouth? Probably not. Well let me tell you, it's damn near impossible. I didn't want to smile, but my canine companion smiled first. So I have taken the gun from my mouth and laid it down. Now I will lay my body down. I'm tired. Can we continue the story later?

Part II

Angels and Devils / Martyrs and Mortals

Chapter 1

Saint Charles, My Father

Man's best friend was staring me in the face when I woke up a couple of hours ago. The hangover wasn't as bad as I thought it would be. Probably by sleeping twenty hours straight, I slept through most of it. And I was real hungry, so my pooch pal and I split a can of Wolf Brand Chili. And here's what I said to him while I was opening the can with a rusty opener: "And neighbor, how long has it been since you had a can of Wolf Brand Chili? Well, that's too long." You know, the old commercial. He was not amused. But he did eat the chili. I even threw in a couple of stale crackers, *pilón*.

When I was nine, my crazy mother went off the deep end. Like I've said, I don't remember the specifics, but part of that process included talking my dad into moving into town. In this case, town was Podesta, which was ten miles from Mineral. To call Podesta a town is a lot like calling a fourteen-foot bass boat a ship. Podesta's population was a grand total of 863. Of course, that was before the Maxwell family moved in. Shortly after moving into our new home — another lease house moved into town by a now defunct oil company — my mother went totally nuts. A nervous breakdown they called it. Do your nerves actually break down? I've often wondered.

All I know is that my father and his brother, Beason, took her to a psychiatric hospital in Victoria, sixty miles away. This was in 1957. Mental hospitals were still referred to as nut houses, funny farms, etc. My brothers and I were the new kids in town and our mother was in the "loony bin." To say we were stigmatized would be a bit of an understatement. And for any of you out there who have forgotten how cruel kids can be, I will refresh your memories.

The little neighborhood we lived in was made up of old lease houses that had been moved into town by different oil companies. The houses all looked alike. Two-bedroom, rectangular, thousand square feet or less, white asbestos-shingled abodes — your basic oil field trash accommodations. Charlie, Bobby and I shared a bedroom. But at least we each had our own bed, which had not always been the case.

The neighborhood — referred to as Podesta Heights by the locals because it sat atop a little knoll — was the domain of twenty-plus kids of all shapes and sizes, but only one color: white. They ran the gamut from the good, the bad, and the ugly. And there were two truly evil souls in the bunch, but it's hard to pick them out of a crowd when you're only nine years old.

Looking back, the good ones were mostly the girls: Peggy, Linda, June, Jeannie, and especially Janie was good; and, as I found out later, bad, in a good kind of way. I have discovered in life that the good ones are usually the girls and women. Women, by nature, are superior to men in virtually every way, except in their capacity to be cruel. I know there are exceptions, such as my mother, but I don't really want to talk about them, if you don't mind. Some of the guys were good too, like Teddy, who would later become my body-guard in junior high and high school. He called me "Sweet Pea."

Then there were Ronnie, Neal, Jimmy, and others whose names I can't remember. The evil ones were brothers: Leroy and Thomas. In between were the ugly ones: Paul, Ricky, Danny, et al., who said things like: "I'm glad my mother's not crazy like yours." "You old son of a nut, you." "Here comes Jamey, his mother's lamey, in the brainy." And so on and so forth.

There was a lady who lived next door who tried to be nice and do what neighbors do when there is a tragedy, which is how my mother's illness was treated by the adults. It might as well have been a death in the family. Mrs. Hopkins would bring food to our house almost every night. She told me if I would go pick some wild mustang grapes down on Medio Creek, she would make me a green grape pie. So I did and she did. The pie tasted good, I think, but mostly I was thankful for her kindness.

My father, I now know, was devastated by my mother's illness. Not because it meant that besides working three jobs he now had total responsibility for three young sons — that was nothing new. And it wasn't because of the shame he was facing for having a crazy wife — I don't think what other people gossiped about really bothered him. It was because he truly loved her. He felt like a failure for not being able to help her. Of course back then, no one could, but he didn't know that. He felt guilty, plain and simple. My father tried his best to shelter us from the truth about my mother's illness. That was an effort in futility, because we were getting the "straight skinny" from our ever-thoughtful friends and neighbors. After several months, dad took us to visit our Mom in the hospital.

Here are the two things I remember about the visit:

First, while my brothers and I were alone in the hospital lobby, we stuffed Kleenex in the coin return of the pay phone. My brothers said we would check it before we left to see what fortunes we had made. It seemed like an excellent plan.

Then, seeing my mom in the hospital bed. She was in her nightgown, her hair sticking out in an odd fashion. She didn't look like Ida Lupino anymore. Have I mentioned that people often told her she looked like Ida Lupino? Maybe that's why my dad loved her. Who knows? Anyway, she was holding a painting she had made during her stay. This was part of her therapy. Even at nine years old I remember thinking what a lousy painting it was. But then again, what should I have expected from a woman whose brain had been fried by several hundred thousand volts of electricity? Of course I didn't know this at the time, but in 1957 shock therapy was the treatment du jour. I understand it's making a comeback. Scary. I don't remember if Charlie or Bobby checked the pay phone when we left. I know I sure didn't.

After four or five months in the mental institution, my mother came home. I'm not sure this was the good news. I had drawn very close to my father. My mother resented this. Not because I wasn't close to her — I never was — but because she felt that she was receiving less than her quota of attention from Charles. Charles, who was working himself into the ground while raising three boys. Charles, who was sleeping about three hours at night when he was lucky. Charles, who never once raised his voice in anger to her. Charles still wasn't doing enough.

Later that year, I remember Mom getting me and my brothers out of bed in the middle of the night. She was leaving my dad. I did not want to go with her. My dad was sitting at the old, chrome-legged, red-Formica-topped dining table. He looked very sad. And it's the first time I realized he was bald. I think it made me love him even more. He was sitting there sad and bald. I ran to him, calling back to my mother, "I want to stay with Daddy." She would have none of that. That might have made things easier for Charles to take. I remember being disappointed that my father did not put up a fight to keep me. I know now that my dad could never stand up to her. It wasn't his fault. He loved her too much.

This little adventure lasted all of two days. We stayed in a run-down motel behind the Bronco Drive-In Theater in Beckville where we three boys sneaked over the fence to watch an old B movie. I think Jayne Mansfield was in it, but I couldn't swear to it. Anyway, it was mom and her three sons staying in one tiny motel room. Cozy. She couldn't take it. We went back home to Charles. He seemed happy to see all of us. I was sure happy to see him.

On November 29, 1957, the event that changed my life happened. It involved Leroy and Thomas, the shit-eating, mother-fucking (pardon my French) Gohlke brothers. I never told anyone about the incident upon penalty of death. The Gohlke brothers swore they would kill me if I ever told a soul. I had no reason to doubt them after seeing what they were capable of doing.

They also said they would tell everyone that I was crazy like my mother. This threat was even more effective. I often wonder what my father would have done to the Gohlke brothers had he known. Probably what I did to three men in Dos Cruces, forty-one years later.

I changed after my ninth birthday. I think most of the changes were internal. To a large extent, I died inside. The funny thing is no one seemed to notice. My parents never commented on it and Charlie and Bobby were busy with their own lives. I had always been quiet and shy at school, so teachers and students were heedless. Only God and I knew I was different. That's when we came to our agreement. You can take God's word to the bank.

Time went on even when life didn't. I went to school, played with other kids, participated in sports and other activities just like a real child would do. As I grew older, I went out with girls, including Janie

Beauchamp, who taught me a few things. On the out-side, life was normal. I was a master of charades.

My Mom got well enough — or at least it appeared so to the general population of Podesta — to get a job. Actually, it became several jobs, since she couldn't keep one very long. She also was a master of charades. I'm sure that's where I got my talent. When I was grown, I had an old girlfriend tell me she had heard my Mom had several affairs, mostly with her bosses. She said everyone in Podesta, except for my dad, knew about the affairs. Charles probably knew in his heart, but he would never have said anything. He was afraid my mother would leave him. After she had reported this information to me, I said this to my old girlfriend: "Thanks for sharing that with me." I didn't mean it.

In high school, I had a serious girlfriend. Her name was Claudette. She was pretty. She was superficial. She was better than nothing. Great criteria for a girlfriend, don't you think? By this point in my life about the only thing I was really interested in was getting the hell out of Dodge — Dodge, in this case, being Podesta, Texas. I got a job at the grocery store when I was fifteen. I saved enough money in two years to pay for my first year of college. I even considered marrying Claudette as an excuse to get out on my own, but sanity prevailed. We broke up. Without going into details, neither she nor I were virgins anymore. She soon fell for a jock on the football team — her being a cheerleader and all. His name was Patrick — a friend of mine, more or less. They got married and probably lived superficially ever after. That might not be so bad.

Charlie and Bobby went to college. Charlie to Texas A&I and Bobby to Southwest Texas State. My parents paid their way. Charlie dropped out after his freshman year and was drafted into the Army. Bobby graduated in four years, and before he was drafted, joined the Air Force. This was during the Vietnam era, but neither of my brothers had to go fight. They put their time in stateside and told me to avoid military duty at all cost.

I graduated in 1966. As I have said, I saved enough to pay for my first year of college. My mother made it clear they couldn't afford to pay for my education. That was fine. I didn't want to owe her anything. My mother always saw to it that Charlie and Bobby had whatever they wanted. But she usually went out of her way to let me know that there was nothing left for me: cars, clothes, Christmas presents, college, etc. I got used to it. I never resented my brothers for what they got. And I don't think they ever really noticed the things I didn't get. No big deal, just life on Jamey Maxwell lane.

After my first year in college, I dropped out and went to work for a seismograph company. Because of my asthma, I had been classified as 1-Y by the local draft board, so I was relatively safe from being inducted into the armed services. I was eighteen years old and away from home as planned. I needed to earn money, not only for college, but to get my bottom four front teeth fixed. They were crooked, and though no one could really see them except me, when I looked in the mirror, they bothered me a lot. They bothered me to this point: one night, when I was still in high school and really drunk, I got out a pair of pliers and tried to pull them myself. I couldn't get a good grip or I might have done it.

I broke down and asked my parents if they would take me to the dentist and have them fixed like they had done for Bobby when he was sixteen. My mother said, "Your father and I don't have the money for that. If you want your teeth fixed, you'll have to get a job and pay for it." My dad said nothing. I expected nothing less. That was the first and last time I asked my parents for anything. Hence, my job with the seismograph company.

Seismograph companies explore for oil. The people who work for them are nomads. And mostly alcoholics. It's a tough life. I was eighteen. The next youngest guy was in his thirties. Most were in their forties, really old, or so I thought at the time. We worked twelve-hour days, six or seven days a week, laying out cable with "jugs." Jugs were electronic measuring devices, therefore the lowly laborers like me were known as "jug hustlers" or "jug stompers." I always thought it had kind of a sadistic, sexual connotation. The jug hustlers would pick up giant spools of rubber-insulated cable and walk for miles down a dusty *sendero* — plowed days before — unspooling the cable. After the cables were laid out and the jugs attached, a small drilling rig would punch sixty-foot holes. We would screw several cans of dynamite together, attach electrical wire, and dropped the charge down the hole. The shooter would then detonate the dynamite. An operator — sitting in a truck filled with seismographic equipment hundreds of yards down the *sendero* — would then print out the results.

We worked in one-hundred-plus-degree temperatures in the summer and twenty-degree temperatures in the winter. I was getting minimum wage, about $1.50 per hour, but with a lot of overtime. After working all day, we would go to our motel rooms, take a shower, and start drinking and playing poker or go barhopping.

We would stay up to 2:00 or 3:00 A.M., get up at 5:00 A.M., and go to work still drunk. The hangover would hit at about 10:00 A.M. or 95 degrees, whichever came first. I would crawl under one of the trucks at lunch for a thirty-minute nap. What a life.

After four months, I had saved enough money to see a dentist. I took off one day from work and had those four pesky teeth pulled. My dad drove me back to Freer, Texas, about 150 miles from Beckville, that evening. I got up at 5:00 the next morning and went to work, my mouth still bleeding. About a month later, the dentist put in a permanent bridge with real-gold backing. My first major accomplishment in life.

After seven months, I had squirreled away enough funds to go back to college for another year. While in college, I worked several jobs. Enough to get me through to graduation. My father attended my graduation ceremonies. My mother, who was drinking excessively then, was too ill to attend. *No problema.* Charles was very proud of me.

Let me finish up about my dad — for now — by saying this: He never once told me he loved me. He never once hugged me. But there was no doubt in my mind, ever, concerning his feeling for me. Love emanated from his pores. He reeked of love. From my father I received all the love I needed — through osmosis.

Chapter 2

Two Angels and a Martyr

After college, I went to work as a sky marshal with the United States Government. A year or so later, I was hired as a Special Agent with the U.S. Customs Service. I know I've told you this already, but please abide me.

In 1974, I met Connie Lee Fitzpatrick. I was twenty-five and she was twenty. She had just come to work as a clerk-stenographer with the Customs Service. The first day I met her, I thought she was a high school student, so I didn't pay that much attention to her, except to note that she was absolutely, drop-dead gorgeous. She was 5' 3", with long, straight, light brown hair, porcelain skin, high cheekbones, big blue eyes, a dazzlingly bright smile, and a body that would stop an entire shop full of clocks. This may sound cliché and chauvinistic, but so be it. It's true. As Mary Poppins might say, "she was practically perfect in every way."

When I found out that Connie Lee was actually twenty years old and a full-time employee, I started finding reasons to hang around her. We bonded almost immediately. We laughed at the same things. We liked the same movies. I could talk to her. For the first time since I was nine years old, I felt a flicker of life inside. The flicker would soon become a flame and then a roaring three-alarm fire. I was in love. But I was still too shy to ask her out. She took care of that. She told me to call her sometime after work. She wasn't nearly as shy as I was, and since she typed all of my reports, my productivity, at least in the paperwork department, went up several hundred percent.

As a Customs Agent, one of my jobs was to work undercover. This usually meant going to a bar with an informant, drinking heavily, and trying to entice bad guys into being bad enough to get arrested. It's a dirty, rotten job, but I volunteered. Bad guys are usually pretty easy to entice. They're usually not too bright and they're always greedy — a potent combination. There's not a lot of future in being a bad guy, unless your idea of a future involves sharing a prison cell with other bad guys, and sometimes, future romantic partners, if you know what I mean and I think you do.

Informants, on the other hand, were almost always harder to deal with than the bad guys. Mainly because informants are usually bad guys who are just a little smarter than the other bad guys. They are sneaky. They are devious. They are notorious liars. And they are always looking for an easy buck.

My number one informant was John "Big John" Duffy. He was 6'3" and weighed at least 250 pounds.

He was big and would do anything to keep from having to work for a living. He was a hell of a snitch, if you could keep him on the right track, but his mind would wander. Nowadays he would be diagnosed with attention deficit disorder. He was a compulsive liar. I don't think he knew it. He just couldn't tell the difference between fact and fiction. Or as Robert Browning said, "He said true things, but called them by wrong names." But he attracted other bad guys like flypaper, which made him an excellent informant.

One particular night, I was in a bar on the north side of Houston, a notorious area for all sorts of riffraff, rabble, scum, down-and-outers, et al. I was with Big John and his sister, Ursula, trying to buy some cocaine from a typical Houston Northside small-timer. My heart and mind were not in it. My heart, mind, and probably other body parts were on Connie Fitzpatrick.

I had consumed six or seven beers and screwed up enough nerve to walk over to the pay phone and give her a call. Much to my surprise, she answered on the first ring. She said she had been expecting my call. Even with the sedation of a six-pack or so, I could still feel my heart skip a beat. I felt alive. Really alive.

We agreed to meet in the parking lot of TGI Friday's in an hour — around 9:00 P.M. I was nervous, but the good kind of nervous. I got there fifteen minutes early, driving my government car, a 1974 Ford Galaxy. She pulled up next to me in her little Volkswagen Beetle and got out of her car dressed in jeans and a solid-yellow halter-top. Her hair was halfway down her back, which was mostly bare. She took my beer-soaked breath away.

I opened the passenger door and she climbed in. I was worried about what to say, but that point was soon moot. Without saying a word, she reached over and kissed me hard and for a long time. I was paralyzed with excitement, apprehension, and lust. She grabbed my hand and placed it on her ample breast. The rest, as they say, is history.

Connie and I dated steadily (every night) for the next two months. I couldn't get enough of her and I think she felt the same way. I told her I loved her and she said "ditto." After two months, she moved in with me. We were inseparable; bosom buddies, so to speak; thick as thieves; quite a pair. For the first time in my life, I felt a woman's love. It was unlike anything I had ever experienced. The only way I could describe it is to say that for the first time in my life I felt real. It was amazing. She had performed a miracle; she had brought me back from the dead. Physically, we couldn't get enough of each other. But we sure as hell tried.

Connie and I were alike in several ways. Until we found each other we were basically alone in the world. Her parents had divorced when she was five years old. Because her mother was in no position, financially, to raise her and her two brothers, the children wound up living with her father. He was a tyrant. In his mind, it was a prerequisite for being a proper father in this dog-eat-dog world.

Her father remarried. Her stepmother had children of her own, so Connie was neglected when she wasn't being resented. Because she was both beautiful and smart, the resentment grew. She withdrew into her own little world. When she graduated from high school, she got the hell out of Dodge, in this case, Dodge being the Fitzpatrick household. Her misfortune became my fortune. I reaped what her father and stepmother had sowed. I was one lucky son-of-a-bitch and I knew it. But somewhere along the way, I forgot just how lucky I was. I paid the ultimate price for my memory lapse. God giveth and God taketh away. God is one tough Son-of-a-Bitch.

After six months of industrial strength love, we decided to get married. Since we just had each other (although I loved my father dearly and she loved her mother dearly, they had their own flounder to fricassee), we decided to have a small wedding — just me and Connie. The two of us, soul mates. We didn't tell another soul.

A justice of the peace in the tiny town of Balcones married us on August 10, 1974. He could not figure out why we came all the way from Houston to get married in Balcones — by him. He was just lucky, I guess. So was I. Shortly after we were married, Customs transferred me to El Paso, Texas. Connie quit her job. We loaded up my Dodge van which I had customized myself and hooked her VW behind it. We put all of our earthly belongings in both vehicles with room to spare. Material things, which didn't mean a thing. We headed west. We felt young, wild, and free. What a feeling. I wish I could feel it again, but I never will.

Working as a Customs Agent in El Paso was much different from working in Houston. Things were more spontaneous. The agents were tougher. The bad guys were badder. It was the wild wild West. In El Paso, we were trying to catch big-time drug smugglers, arms dealers, often Mexican State and Federal Police, gold smugglers, and various and sundry other crooks. The Texas-Mexican border is rugged country with rugged and often ragged people. What an experience. Rapidly, I was losing my naïveté.

Often, much too often, when a smuggler was caught crossing the border from Mexico with illegal drugs, usually cocaine and heroin, they would swallow them. Many times the drugs were inside balloons or condoms. When this happened, the Customs Agents on duty would have to rush to one of the international bridges, arrest the suspect and go directly to the hospital. The lucky doctor on duty would either pump their stomachs or administer drugs that would cause the perpetrator to pass the drugs — orally or anally. Then the duty agent would get to search for the stuff, hoping like hell to find them in a condom. Puke or shit, what's your pleasure?

In El Paso, as in Houston, I felt the need to prove myself to the other guys. I had long hair, unlike the other guys; was still skinny, by far the youngest agent in El Paso; plus I didn't look very tough. I was always the first out of the car, the first through the door, the first to draw a weapon, the first to put cuffs on the "perps."

After some initial skepticism, I quickly earned my supervisors' and fellow agents' respect. Again, this was out of fear of disgracing myself, rather than my being a paragon of bravery. But they couldn't tell the difference. Cool.

I became especially close to a veteran agent named Al Pearson. "Big Al" looked just like Earl Campbell, the Hall-of-Fame running back with the Houston Oilers. He was about forty years old, the strong, silent type, and was particularly feared by the bad guys we came across. To them, he projected this image: "I want you to give me a reason to hurt you."

One day, Big Al and I were taking two perps from the El Paso County Jail to be arraigned in federal court. It was standard operating procedure for us to handcuff prisoners when taking them the two blocks to the courthouse. For some reason, Al had forgotten to bring his handcuffs. He looked at his prisoner and said with a straight face and a low growl, "If you run, I'll kill you." We had no trouble with either prisoner. Even I walked a little more slowly.

In reality, Al was a pussycat (a pussycat on steroids) and very funny. He kind of took me under his wing, showed me the ropes, gave me a clue. We did a lot of late night drinking and talking in bars and strip joints. That was part of our job description — looking for the bad guys, you know. It was tough. Anyway, I learned that Al's ambition was to retire to East Texas, buy 10 acres with an old house to fix up, and garden until he died. He and his wife, Ruby, had no kids. I lost touch with Al over the years. I hope he had the chance to realize his dreams. For me, it's only been nightmares.

After working in El Paso for five years, I was promoted to Supervisory Special Agent back in the Houston Regional Office. I was still only thirty years old, a rising star, a young man on his way up, yadda,

yadda, yadda. Connie was still a mere child of twenty-five. We had no children yet, but we were sure working on it. The year was 1979. We were crazy in love. We still had the Dodge van and VW, but this time it took a Mayflower truck to haul our earthly belongings back to Houston.

Julie Marie, our oldest daughter, was born in 1980. I can't begin to tell you how happy and proud I was. We had expected a boy the first time out, since that was the trend on the Maxwell side of the family. A boy would have been great too. But by this stage of my life, I had been drawing toward the inevitable conclusion that the female of the species is superior in essentially every way, especially in the domain of morality.

I had spent enough time around men, particularly of the Special Agent variety, to realize that most of them, including me, were lower than whale shit. Hence the joke: What's the difference between a man and a catfish? Answer: One's a scum-sucking bottom-feeder and the other one's a fish. Anyway, Connie Lee had lit the fire of life inside me, and my beautiful new daughter made it dance and swirl with delight.

In 1982, we hit the jackpot again. Josie Ellen was born. Josie, my sweet little Josie.

As our two daughters grew, it became apparent that Julie would be the serious one, like her mother, and Josie would be the devil-may-care type, like me. They were both smart and pretty, but Julie was moody. When she was in a good mood, she was fun and funny. When she was in a bad mood, *cuidado*. Josie, on the other hand, was almost always happy. She would go out of her way to make me and her mom feel good, even when she was a tyke of three or four. What a blessing.

Julie was the tomboy, my sports buddy. Josie was the little princess. Always dressing up, putting on make-up, being feminine. I loved them both dearly — on the same scale, but in different ways. I miss them more than you will ever know and beyond my capacity to explain. Connie, too. Fathers should never outlive their children. Husbands should never outlive their wives. I guess I really haven't. For all intents and purposes, I died the same day they did. As Julie grew older, she grew prettier. She complained that her beautiful hair was frizzy. Every day was a bad hair day as far as she was concerned. She had green eyes; white skin, with just the right amount of freckles; perfect teeth (after $3,000 worth of orthodontist bills); and a cute little nose right in the middle of her face.

At fifteen, she went from being skinny to being slender. From being pretty to being beautiful. Her metamorphosis to womanhood was only a year or two away. She didn't make it. She used to say, "Daddy, I have your toes." Or, "Daddy, I have your ears." My reply was always the same, "Well, give 'em back!" She always giggled. We were connected by more than blood — we were joined at the soul. She was and is my angel.

Josie was born with light brown hair that gradually turned blonde. Her eyes were blue, bluer than Frank Sinatra's. From birth she was beautiful, inside and out. She had her mother's genes — every one of them. Her eyes always sparkled. By the time Josie turned thirteen, her smile was lethal to boys, with no known antidote. She was perfection made mortal. Josie could converse with adults by the time she was five. She could be sincere or facetious depending on which way the discussion was going. Her comedic timing was always impeccable.

And this was how sweet she was: when she turned twelve, I decided that she was too old to be tucked in bed at night. She said, "That's okay Daddy, I'll tuck you and Mom in from now on." For the last year of her life she did just that, without fail. She was joy personified.

And always there was Miss Connie Lee Maxwell, *nee* Fitzpatrick. The love of my life. My reason for being. When she died, she had just turned forty-two. She had actually become more ravishing as she grew older — genetics I guess. Connie Lee was not always easy to get along with; she could be a perfectionist and demanding at times, but she could also be the kindest, sweetest, and most caring mother and wife ever to grace this earth. I never called her Connie, only Honey or Sweetheart. I love you, Honey. I miss you, Sweetheart. You were a martyr to my selfishness and stupidity. And I am so, so sorry.

Chapter 3

Angelita (Little Angel)

My father died in 1997, about six months before my wife and daughters. My mother had vacated earth three years earlier after spending two long years in a nursing home. She was only sixty-one but had the self-inflicted body of a ninety-year old when my brothers and I committed her to the Golden Years Retirement Cottage. Talk about your false advertising, Golden Years looked more like piss-yellow years. Retirement meant death and the cottage was more like a barracks. But that was all we could afford.

Charles couldn't make himself go visit her. We, my brothers and I, didn't blame him. We told him to get on with his life. But, until she died, he couldn't. My brothers and I talked about this many times. How could he possibly love this woman? Maybe he loved her because she looked like Ida Lupino. Maybe he loved her because he had lost all of his hair while still in high school and she was the only girl who showed any interest in him. Maybe he loved her because he understood she was born to a loveless and dysfunctional family and he thought he could overcome this by loving her too much. Maybe it was just a case of unexplainable true love. True love is a motherfucker sometimes. We handled all of the nursing home arrangements and the funeral when the time came.

My father grieved for two years before finding a female friend in Dos Cruces. I think it was just platonic, but I wouldn't swear to it, and I hope not. Her name was Lucy and she was several years older than him. He was sixty-nine. They enjoyed each other's company. She was kind to him — treated him like he was important. A new experience for Charles. For hours, he would sit and tell stories and she would listen quietly, never interrupting. After a while, I'm sure tales were being recycled, but she never seemed to mind. Lucy had been a widow for more than twenty years. It was a symbiotic relationship. What more can you ask for in this life.

Did I tell you how my dad wound up in Dos Cruces? I don't think I did. Well, here's the Reader's Digest version: The little oil company my father worked for in Mineral was bought out by a bigger company which in turn was bought out by an even bigger company. The law of nature, survival of the fittest and all that jazz. In 1973, after twenty-some-odd years in the same job, he was laid off. He was downsized before downsizing was even in our vocabulary. He had been a completely loyal employee, missing a total of three days of work when he was badly burned on the job, in twenty-plus years. Now he was unemployed. "Thank you Charles for all of your hard work and dedication, and, if you don't mind, kiss our big fat stinking corporate ass." As a wise man, or wise guy, once said, "No good deed goes unpunished." Charles was devastated. Marlena, my mother, blamed him. Said it must have been something he had said. Or maybe something he had done or didn't do. Charlie, Bobby, and I consoled him as much as we could, but we were all busy with our own little adventures.

I wish now that I could have been more comfort to him. What I did do, though, that Charles never found out about, was call Houston Production Service, the corporation that laid him off. I told the vice-president of personnel what a great big bag of cockroach shit I thought he and his company were. It made me feel a little better.

The good news was this: after being unemployed for a couple of months, a guy my dad knew called and told him that a company was looking for a gauger to take care of ten new wells in Dos Cruces on a contract basis. This meant that Charles would now be self-employed.

He was apprehensive at first, but his three sons convinced him to take the leap. He did. He soon got several contracts with other companies due to his well-earned reputation of being honest and hard working. Soon he was taking care of fifty-two wells in and around Dos Cruces. His three sons were very proud of their father. His wife, now that was a different story.

My dad's unexpected success was perceived as a threat by my mother. She couldn't stand it. She would berate him about anything and everything — attack him personally. She went into overdrive with her drinking. She threatened to kill him. My brothers and I (my father couldn't bear to do it) had her admitted to the state hospital in San Antonio to dry out. She blamed Charles and me for doing this to her. She never forgave us.

After she got out, she was a lot more subtle with her campaign to destroy Charles. It was more like guerrilla warfare. She had her ways. But dad survived until she went into the nursing home. He felt guilty for everything that my mother went through, of course. We could never take that away from him. We had quit trying long ago.

About the time Charles met Lucy, he was confronted with an unexpected opportunity. One of the companies my dad contracted with was selling off its wells in Texas, including six around Dos Cruces. They were asking the salvage price for the wells. That is, just the value of the old equipment, which wasn't much: $55,000. Again, Charles was apprehensive. But again his three boys talked him into pulling the trigger on the deal. We helped get him the loan and set up his little office in his little house.

The last year of my father's life — before his first and last heart attack — was extraordinary. His friend, Lucy, treated him like the King of Dos Cruces. He started Maxwell and Sons Oil and Gas with six gas wells, which netted him about $3,000 a month. A king's ransom for the King of Dos Cruces. We called him an oil and gas tycoon. He loved it. Dad gave up taking care of wells for other companies, which gave him time to spend with his seven grandchildren, which was his favorite thing to do. And I think he was finally getting over the unfounded guilt he felt about my mother. Then he died. Our father, King Charles of Dos Cruces, had a massive heart attack. What a way to go. Charles checked out at the apex of his life. If only we could all say that.

We had the funeral in Catarino, which is the county seat of Losoya County, thirty miles from Dos Cruces. My brothers and I buried Charles in the Dos Cruces cemetery. We thought this fitting since Dos Cruces is the place where my dad finally found a little peace and happiness in his otherwise shit-filled world. My mother had been buried back in Beckville. We wanted Charles to be able to actually rest in his final resting place, if you get my drift.

One other thing: I have told you that Dos Cruces is a harsh, drab, reddish brown and beige world. That's true, with one splendid exception: the cemetery. Although the Dos Cruces cemetery is right on the edge of town, it lies just over a small ridge. I had never seen it until the day my father was buried. There are the usual tombstones and grave markers and a few large monuments: angels and children. But here's the thing: the Dos Cruces cemetery is in vividly surreal Technicolor. Virtually every grave is adorned with plastic flowers of bright reds, yellows, blues, oranges, purples and so on. It's a Salvador Dali dreamscape painted by Leroy Neiman. It's a faux Disney World underworld. It's the Garden of Eden on acid. Talk about mixed emotions. It's hard to be too somber (or sober for that matter) in a, get this: fetid field festooned with fabulous fake flowers.

Unbelievably, my father had made out a will before he died. My brothers and I were shocked. We just couldn't picture him sitting down and writing a will. He had provided that everything he owned would be divided equally among his three sons, including Maxwell and Sons Oil and Gas. But Charlie, Bobby, and I all had good jobs. Our families were settled. Kids in school. There was nothing in Dos Cruces for any of us. We all had our own perch to parch. Things would change six months later.

Fortunately, instead of selling Maxwell and Sons Oil and Gas, along with dad's little one bedroom clapboard house, we hired a gauger from Dos Cruces to take care of the six wells and rented the house to a local, elderly couple. It's almost like God had a plan. Hmm.

The day my wife and daughters were killed in the car wreck, I was fucking another woman. Her name doesn't matter. And it wasn't making love or having sex — it was fucking. By that time in my life, I had been severely depressed for many years. For a long time, Connie had tried to persuade me to see some kind of doctor — any kind. She had read about new, effective antidepressants like Prozac. She knew I was suffering — saw it coming long before I did. She was aware of my mother's mental history.

I refused to admit I was susceptible to my mother's defectiveness. Plus, I had been promoted to Assistant Regional Director of Investigations in Houston. I didn't have time to be depressed and I refused to show any sign of weakness to myself. What a fool.

At home, I had become quiet and withdrawn. I was

edgy, snapping at Connie and the girls for no good reasons. This worried Julie and Josie. They didn't understand. Connie was beginning to suffer because of my illness. Finally, she convinced me to see a doctor. The first guy I saw diagnosed it as a stress-related disorder. He prescribed medication that had little or no positive effects and several negative ones. I quit taking it after a couple of weeks. When things got worse, I agreed to see a shrink. He prescribed Prozac, which helped almost immediately. Connie and the girls noticed the difference before I did. I took it for a year, felt much better, then with my warped logic decided since I felt so good, I didn't need it anymore. As Bugs Bunny would say, "What a maroon!"

I didn't tell Connie I had quit taking my Prozac, but she noticed soon enough. I told her I quit because I didn't like the side effects. She knew better. She said she hated it when I pulled my "macho bullshit" routine. That was a pretty apt description.

It wasn't long before I was looking to other outlets for relief from my depression. For a while, it was booze. But, of course, that only made me feel worse — upon sobering up. Then I decided my wife really didn't understand me. Ladies, have you heard that one before? I struck up a "friendship" with a woman at work. She was pretty screwed-up too, which reinforced the attraction. She understood me. She had been there. She really cared. Blah, blah, blah. The devil in disguise? Not really. Just another fucked-up person like me, who happened to come along at just the wrong time. Did God send her? Was it a test? If so, I flunked . . . with devastating consequences.

I don't remember the funeral. My brothers and their wives were there to help. They did their best, assisting with the funeral arrangements, trying to console me, etcetera. The only thing I insisted upon was closed caskets.

After the funeral, my brother took me back to our house. Mine and Connie Lee's and Julie's and Josie's house. It was no longer the home that Connie had made for all of us, with her impeccable taste and little touches of love everywhere. Although the house was full of well meaning people, as far as I was concerned, it was empty. So was I. No grief or guilt. Not yet. Only a void. A black hole. I was a zombie. The walking dead.

People said things to me. I know, that's what people do. But I don't remember one word of comfort or one word period. God was there, I think. I felt His presence. He was neither consoling nor mocking. He was just there. I'm not sure why. He certainly wasn't welcome.

I submitted my resignation at work one week after the funeral. I was forty-seven years old with twenty-five years of federal law enforcement. I wasn't old enough for full retirement benefits, but I could not have cared less. Sixty percent of my current salary was more than enough money for what I had planned. Plus, I had $550,000 in life insurance from my wife and daughters — blood money.

But where I was going, trade was conducted in a distinctly different currency. The wages of sin are death, the legal tender being guilt, pain, and suffering. Based on that, I had quite a nest egg. In Hell, I would be a wealthy son-of-a-bitch.

I had a few things to take care of first. Some loose ends to tie up. My brothers suggested I move to Dos Cruces, to my dad's little shanty, to recoup. Or as Bobby said, "You need to go get all your shit in one basket." Then Charlie said, "Yeah, and you need to get your turds in a row." I love my brothers. They have such a way with words. So off to Dos Cruces I went. That was three years ago. I'm still here. Not sure why. Not sure how much longer.

Strange things are commonplace in Dos Cruces. Is that an oxymoron? If so, it's only one of many in this little Twilight Zone. *Por ejemplo*, after my dad died, for a week or so, while my family and I were there, on a daily basis various knickknacks, trinkets, and trifles showed up on the tiny front porch of his tiny domicile. Little ceramic frogs, costume jewelry, indiscernible articles made of tin foil, rocks and sticks, and other unidentified fuzzy objects (UFOs). After a couple of days, they began to resemble a shrine. Each object a separate totem. Somebody was trying to tell some-body something. I think it was a tribute to Saint Charles, my father. After the weirdness wore off, it was kind of nice.

When I moved into St. Charles Place, guess what started showing up on the tiny porch. Yep. More totems. I never saw or heard anyone at the front door. For the first week, I would wake up in the morning and there would be a new alm. Many towns have their welcome wagons. This, I guess, was the Dos Cruces version. Interesting.

Angelita Cavazos was the first person I met after I

migrated to Dos Cruces. She worked in her grand-mother's restaurant, Reynaldo's Place. Not sure who Reynaldo was or if he even existed. Dora Cavazos was Angelita's grandmother. She was in her late forties going on sixty. Life is hard on people in Dos Cruces. *No misericordia*. No mercy. Dora was fat and jovial and although the words fat and jovial are often used in the same sentence, it's been my experience that is not always the case.

I had come to the restaurant — let's say bar — for a beer. I had been in Dos Cruces about two weeks and had yet to leave my new *casa*. This was my first out-ing. I had drunk myself sober many times during those first two weeks. I didn't feel like socializing, but I did feel like escaping my new prison for a short while and maybe having another beer.

A young girl, who was thirteen going on twenty, walked over and said, "Hi, I'm Angelita (she said this with a cute lilt, Ahn-hey-lee-tah, the Spanish pronun-ciation), what's your name?" "I'm Jamey Maxwell," I halfheartedly replied. "Oh, you're Carlos' son. Everyone in Dos Cruces loved Carlos. *Un hombre amable*. A very nice man." This touched me. And I thought I was untouchable.

"I will call you Jaime, she bubbled. That's Mexican for James."

"Okay, I'll call you Little Angel. That's gringo for Angelita." I shot back.

She giggled and giggled. She sounded like Josie. God and Jesus help me.

For the next couple of years, I became a regular at Reynaldo's, as most Dos Cruces residents were. You're probably wondering, "Why was he still around? After all, hadn't he come to Dos Cruces to end it all? But, I think you know the answer: God wasn't through with me yet. I got to know Angelita fairly well. I watched her blossom into womanhood and thought of my own little angel, Julie, and how she never quite made it that far.

Angelita, like most young girls in Dos Cruces, was growing up fast. Too fast. She was very pretty. Not quite beautiful, but the cream of the crop in Dos Cruces. And, disturbingly to me, she was honing her flirting skills to a point far beyond where her limited life experiences had prepared her. But she was a lady in waiting. What was she waiting for? To get the hell out of Dodge, in this case, Dodge being Dos Cruces, Texas, of course.

All young people here were trying to escape their personal prisons. The isolation, the backwardness, the hopelessness known as Dos Cruces. For us older folk, Dos Cruces was just fine. We were going nowhere. Except maybe to Hell, in some of our cases.

But Angelita was smarter than your average bear. She wanted out very badly. Her Hell was Dos Cruces. Her mother had abandoned her when Little Angel was a baby. She never knew her father. Never knew her mother for that matter. Her mother had simply disappeared from the face of the earth, for all intents and purposes. Little Angel was smart enough to know the future, her future, did not exist in D.C., as she referred to Dos Cruces.

But the only marketable skills she possessed were her prettiness and her flirtiness. She intended to use them to their maximum potential. It got her killed.

And I never said a word. Never warned her. Never tried to stop her. Never tried to tell her the ways of the world. I thought just being nice to her was enough. I was too busy wallowing in my own guilt and self-pity. Another merit badge on my way to becoming one of Hell's Boy Scouts.

Chapter 4

Daniel, the Goatboy

I told you earlier that I was the only person in Dos Cruces who didn't have a personal vendetta against grass. I am a pacifist in this regard. I also coexist with weeds and other noxious plants. Consequently, my yard quickly became overgrown. Believe me when I say I didn't give a shit. Because my soul was a thicket of guiltweed, I was oblivious to the jungle around me. But that didn't mean the other denizens of Dos Cruces weren't mindful of my untidiness. A knock on my door one hot spring morning hoisted me from my Miller Lite-induced stupor. It was Borrego. Daniel Galván, the goatboy. Now, in the Spanish language *borrego* can mean a couple of things. It can mean a lamb. Or it can mean a person who is slow, mentally. In Daniel's case, both meanings fit. Daniel is special. Daniel is a lamb that loves goats. He was grinning from ear to ear. Daniel is about 5′ 6″, maybe 140 pounds, and dark-skinned.

He walks with a slight limp. His hair is eternally tasseled and his front teeth are crooked (my sympathies). Even with these imperfections, he was a joy to behold.

I knew Daniel from my visits to Reynaldo's. He helped Dora clean and sweep the place. He also washed dishes when Huero, the regular dishwasher, was too hung over to show up. Daniel mimed pushing a lawnmower back and forth. I smiled even though I didn't feel like it. Chronologically, Daniel was probably thirty-five, maybe even forty years old. Mentally, Daniel was a boy of five or six. He seemed to experience life on a joyful plane unavailable to most humans. He was truly one of God's own. His bliss was contagious to anyone who had a heart, even a zombie like me. My heart was withered, but apparently not dead.

I said to him in my best Tex-Mex, which isn't that good, "*Bueno, Daniel. Te pago diez dólares. Cuidado. Es posible javelinas allí.*" (Basically, I said, "Okay, Daniel. I will pay you ten dollars. Be careful. There might be javelinas in there.")

Daniel laughed. He kept laughing and repeating "*javelinas allí, javelinas allí.*" Daniel not only got the joke, but he liked it. We were friends.

Daniel lived alone in a tiny shanty behind his parents' slightly larger shanty. His shack did not have running water. It did have a dirt floor. The outhouse was shared by Daniel, his parents, several brothers (I never did get an accurate count) and at least one sister. The entire Galván compound consisted of an acre or so, with the two old, weathered, gray, wooden shacks;

several old outbuildings in various states of disrepair, patched with old metal signs (worth more than the buildings without a doubt); a few really old abandoned vehicles, including a Model-T Ford; some old falling-down, rusted barbed wire fences; and goats. Daniel's goats. Twenty or so, in all of the shapes, colors, and sizes that Spanish goats (a breed that's actually a hybrid) come in.

To say that Daniel loved his goats would be an accurate, but understated, inference. They were, and still are, his life. Daniel kept the newborns in his little dwelling at night to protect them from dogs and coyotes, as well as bad weather. If I had to guess, he slept with them. Because of this, and because people (mostly boys and men) can be heartless, Daniel was not only known as Borrego. I hesitate to tell you this, but I think it's important so that you can understand Daniel's predicament. The *pachucos* (hoodlums and other bad boys) called him *chingador de cabras* (fucker of goats). Goatfucker. Daniel laughed when they said this to his face, but it was more of an embarrassed chuckle. Then he would quickly walk away with his eyes on the Dos Cruces dirt.

I think Daniel had been abused in many ways, by many people, throughout his life. This is more than a layman's guess on my part. I do have experience, not purposely attained, in this field. I could see it in his eyes. I could hear it in his laugh. Maybe that's why I liked him so much. Maybe that's why I agreed to help him at a time when I couldn't even help myself. Daniel is one of God's angels — a cherub actually. More than likely God appointed me as Daniel's part-time, temporary, guardian pseudo-angel. I'm not fit to be a permanent member of God's dominion, but I do odd jobs for Him from time to time.

Chapter 5

Los Diablos (The Devils)

I had seen their kind before. Many times in many places. From Podesta, to Houston, to El Paso, to Dos Cruces, to the various burghs, towns, and cities that lay between. Not only do angels and mortals walk this earth, but likewise, pure evil stalks. In this case a three-pack of pure evil: Luther Axelrod, Dwayne DuBois, and Jacinto "Chango" Ocala. I first became acquainted with their putrid presence at Reynaldo's. It was about two years ago. I was sitting at my usual table, alone, and tranquilized.

I had been in Dos Cruces for a year. This was my routine: walk from St. Charles Place to Reynaldo's at around seven o'clock in the evening, stay until 9 P.M. or six beers, whichever came first, then stumble back home. Six days a week. Reynaldo's was closed on Sundays. I sat by myself, only speaking when spoken to, by Dora, Angelita, or Daniel. Even gregarious Angelita knew I wasn't much into conversation at this stage of my life.

When I arrived each evening, she would say hi, maybe pass on the latest gossip or a little about her plans to blow this Popsicle stand. Then she would bring my beer until I reached my limit. For the most part, people left me alone. My story was known in Dos Cruces. Poor Jamey Maxwell. *Pobrecito*. He lost his family and now he's crazy. *Está loco*. Dos Cruces was where I belonged. I was accepted. I had found my home.

One particularly cold winter's night — you might say a cold night in Hell — two years ago, I met Los Diablos. They did not call themselves Los Diablos. That moniker was bestowed two years later by Violet. Even though she is mute, she is apparently mute in at least two languages. But as an angel, I guess she can communicate in whatever tongue or tongues God favors. Let me say this, Violet's name for these three, this unholy trinity, was right as rain. They were The Devils.

Let me start with the first night I met them. It was around 8:30 P.M. I had been meditating at my corner cubbyhole since seven. Angelita was waiting on tables. There were two other customers — a couple of deer hunters. I could barely see them because they were wearing their camouflage hunting gear. In the kitchen, Dora was cooking and Daniel was washing dishes. All was quiet in Dos Cruces. All was well. Then they arrived. Bad news. Trouble in River City. Diablos in D.C.

When they opened the front door, a blast of arctic air slithered in ahead of them. A chill permeated the dining room and its occupants. Even the hunters faltered from telling their tall tales to look up at what the proverbial cat had dragged in. Of course, I didn't know their names at the time, but I will describe the troika to you.

Luther Axelrod, the leader, strutted in first. Dwayne DuBois held the door open for Luther as a vassal would for a lord. Trailing Luther was Jacinto Ocala, nicknamed Chango (monkey). Ape would have been more apropos. Chango was no more than five feet seven inches tall, but he weighed at least two-fifty. He wasted a lot of space in this world. He was probably thirty years old. Corpulent. Blubbery. A fat motherfucker.

Dwayne (Luther called him "Doobie" in view of his last name) brought up the rear. Dwayne appeared to have a lot of experience doing just that. He was in his mid-twenties. He was short and thin and weasel-like. Stringy, dirty, dishwater blonde hair, acne-scarred face, no lips. Immediately, I was reminded of a remora, one of those little fish that uses suction to attach itself to a shark's back or stomach. Then it just hangs around and feeds off the leavings. In this case, Luther was the shark and Dwayne had used suction to attach himself to Luther's ass.

Dwayne was a toady, a groupie, a wanna-be, a dick-licker, ad nauseum. Dwayne was a "Doobie." He was at Luther's leisure. He would do, and did, essentially anything Luther told him to do. In the end, it got the poor bastard — this ignoble knave, this boorish blackguard, this fetid fool, this sack of syphilitic sala-mander shit — abolished and sent to Hell, where he is now, no doubt, Satan's toady. As if Satan needed another one.

Luther was a piece of work. Begrudgingly, I will say he was a fairly handsome man — in a sinister fashion. Thirty-five or forty years old. He had dark, slicked-back, greasy hair. A throwback to the fifties. His eyes, almost black, were penetrating. They commanded attention. Luther was about six feet tall and slender. Serpentine. I had no trouble picturing him as one of the three original inhabitants of the Garden of Eden, and I think you know the one I mean. His face was tan with a ruddy tint from years of working in the oil fields. A tool pusher on a drilling rig. Chango and Doobie were his charges. His minions. They were roughnecks. He was *el jefe*, the boss.

The three worked for Dawkins Drilling and had been in the Dos Cruces area for a year or so. They were drilling gas wells, mostly wildcatting, for several start-up, investor-owned, and usually investor-screwed, oil and gas companies.

Here is the way investor-owned oil and gas companies worked: two or three guys, almost always including an engineer and/or a geologist, would quit larger companies hoping to hit the big time. They would pick an area they were somewhat familiar with and convince unwary investors — by appealing to the greed in all of us — to fork up some dough to go exploring for black gold (oil) and clear gold (gas). These funds, commonly known as OPM (other people's money), would not only pay for the cost of drilling wells, but all of the salaries and all of the expenses of the engineer and/or geologist, regardless of whether the company brought in a barn burner or crapped out with a dry hole.

In addition, if the company got so lucky as to actually strike oil or gas, the engineer and/or geologist would get a sizable percentage of the well — 10% to 20% or more if they could pull it off. It was a no-lose proposition for the two or three entrepreneurial types who put the OPM together. Rumor has it that on occasion, the two or three guys who put together these start-up, investor-owned companies would sell considerably more than 100% interest in a proposed wildcat well. Follow me on this: if they made a well, all of the investors would get a copy of the ownership of the well. It wouldn't be too difficult to do the math and find out somebody, in this case, the investors, had been screwed. If it was a dry hole, nobody would be that interested in who owned what, because naught times five or ten percent is still naught. So logic dictates, in these cases, a dry hole would be a much better option (since the two or three entrepreneurs got their money up front) and a much safer option (since they wouldn't get sent to the hoosegow). Make sense? I thought so.

Back to the business at hand, Los Diablos. That first night went like this: the three of them sat at the table closest to the bar. They all had their eyes on Angelita. She was only fourteen years old. Los Diablos couldn't have cared less. Old enough to bleed, old enough to breed. I was watching them out of the corner of my eye. My instincts and twenty-five years of experience as a federal agent said *peligroso* (danger). My intuition was right on target. Luther was definitely the brains of the bunch and here is what he was thinking: Catarino, the county seat and location of Sheriff Arlen Buckner's office, was thirty miles — and thirty light years — away. There was no constable or deputy located in Dos Cruces. Dos Cruces was a lawless town in the literal sense.

Luther was the type to make these kinds of cold calculations. Luther was convinced he could do whatever he pleased to whomever he pleased. While he was here, it was his town. Or so he thought. What Luther Axelrod had not counted on that night was the fact that there was another entity in Reynaldo's that was colder than him. Much colder. Me.

Then Angelita proceeded to do something that I feared she would do. She started flirting. Mostly with Luther. She had on a bright red dress — much too short, much too tight. Her black hair hung halfway down her back. Little Angel, who for some reason thought she was so worldly, was so guileless. She didn't have a clue. But she would get a clue, posthaste.

She walked over to their table and said, "Hi. My name is Angelita (Ahn-hey-lee-ta). What's yours?" She was looking straight at Luther. Luther grinned. Easy prey. "My name is Luther, but since I have now had the pleasure of making your acquaintance, just call me Lucky." Angelita giggled. Dwayne tittered. Chango guffawed and said, "*Jefe*, you're so full of shit." Luther replied, "Thank you, thank you very much," in his best Elvis voice, which I admit was pretty good. Everybody chuckled.

"Lucky, you smell pretty good. What ya got on?" Angelita asked. I saw this one coming. Luther laughed, looked at Dwayne and Chango for effect, and said, "Well, little lady, I have a hard on, but I'm surprised you could smell it."

Dwayne and Jacinto cackled. Angelita was startled. She was not familiar with this kind of kidding around. She did not know how to play this game and she didn't really want to learn, at least with these three. In an instant, Angelita had become an adult. She wasn't ready but that didn't matter now. Angelita tried to put the genie back in the bottle, but of course it was too late. She pretended that she didn't get Luther's crude joke. But Little Angel's eyes gave her away. They showed fear. Big mistake. Sign of weakness. Angelita, confused and afraid, retreated to the kitchen and asked her grandmother to wait on the three new patrons. Dora came out and meekly approached their table.

Luther said, "Hi, *Mamacita*. We sure are a horny, I mean hungry, bunch of guys. I hope what we want is on the menu." Dora nervously asked, "What can I get you?" To which Luther replied, "We want the sheepherders' supper." Dora foolishly asked, "What is that, Señor?"

"A glass of goat's milk and a piece of ewe, Mama." The trio laughed. With this, Little Angel bravely returned from the kitchen with Daniel behind her. She spoke up, "Grandma, go back to the kitchen. I'll take care of it."

Daniel was grinning big time but I could tell he was frightened. It was as if he was trying to grin this bad thing away. (Been there, done that, didn't work.) His own instincts were kicking in. *Cuidado.*

Angelita pleaded, "Please, you guys, we don't want any trouble. Just tell me what I can get you."

Dwayne started to say, "I just want a..."

"Shut the fuck up, Doobie," snapped Luther.

"Ahn-hey-lee-ta," Luther mimicked, "I want you to sit in my lap and then we can talk about the first thing that pops up. How does that sound?"

"Please, sir, just let me bring you some beer or something," Angelita's voice quivered.

Chango said, "Bring us three Bud Lights, I'm buying."

"That's mighty white of you," quipped Luther. More chuckles.

Little Angel seemed to be somewhat relieved by this temporary reprieve, but believe me, it was temporary. She quickly turned and walked away.

She returned with beers, and holding her body as far away from the table as possible, stretched to put the bottles down. By this time, they were engaged in some inane, and I'm sure profane, conversation. She withdrew behind the counter and began to pour salt and pepper into their respective shakers. The two semi-invisible deer hunters briskly got up, left their money on the table, and disappeared through the front door.

Luther was the type to not miss a thing; to instinctively survey his surroundings, probing for breaches and faults which he could exploit. Daniel, the goat-boy, had already caught his eye. Luther waved him over to their table. The grin on Daniel's face reformed into a grimace. Poor Daniel. *Pobrecito.* Furtively, and wearily, I watched this debacle unfold. Intervention would soon be required, but I didn't think my heart was up to it. Fear was not a factor on my part. What's the worst they could do to me? Kill me? *Qué le hace.*

What unfolded next would have so much significance and such tragic consequences, but there was no way for me to know this (or was there?) at the time. In retrospect, I think Luther — with a little help from his maleficent master — knew just what he was doing. Luther Axelrod was programming Daniel Galván to confess to the murder of Angelita Cavazos. A murder that wouldn't take place for two more years.

Luther pulled out a chrome and red vinyl chair and patted the seat. Daniel understood. He sat down between Chango and Luther. I could see Luther whispering to Daniel. Chango had his back to me. Dwayne was watching Luther. Daniel was smiling and nodding; smiling and nodding. But I saw pure dread in his eyes.

Then Luther motioned toward Angelita. Daniel turned and looked, still nodding and smiling. Luther touched Daniel on the arm to regain his attention. Then the cocksucking, son of a whore, did this: with the thumb and index finger of his left hand he made a circle, then he rapidly moved his right index finger in and out of this circle — the universal sign for fucking. With his evil, piercing eyes on Daniel he kept repeating the gesticulations until Daniel finally imitated him. Luther grinned a shit eating grin. So did Daniel.

Luther then made a gesture that made my tired blood run cold. With his right index finger extended, he drew it across his throat — the universal sign for murder. Again he repeated the movements until

Daniel copied him. When Daniel finally did duplicate the gesture, Luther pointed to Angelita, laughed, and patted Daniel on the back. Daniel, the goatboy, had a new friend. The Devil.

I should have stepped in and stopped this perverse little sideshow much sooner. Add it to the list of things I should have done but didn't do to earn my eternal salvation. But my body was bone-tired, my mind consumed with grief, and what was left of my soul lay torpid. How's that for a shitty excuse?

Luther Axelrod made the same mistake twice: he underestimated me. The first time was the first night I saw him. It didn't really surprise me. In fact, I readily accepted it. People had been doing it all my life. And I have to admit, that night at Reynaldo's, when I first made the acquaintances of Dwayne DuBois, Jacinto Ocala, and the nefarious Mr. Luther Axelrod, I must have looked totally harmless. Even I thought I was. But we were all wrong.

As an Assistant Special Agent in Charge with the U.S. Customs Service Field Office in Houston, I was a popular supervisor. When I got promoted to Special Agent in Charge (SAC) of the Houston Field Office, I was a popular supervisor. And when I got promoted to the Houston Regional Office as Assistant Regional Director (ARD), I was a popular supervisor. People wanted to work for me. Here's why: I treated people with decency and respect. Simple concept. I wonder why more bosses don't try it? The answer, I think, is this: most of them are total assholes.

There are always a few folks who think because you are nice, they can take advantage. In my years as a supervisor, there were two times that I had to take action because of people taking advantage. Both were Special Agents working under me. The first time I was the SAC in Houston.

One of my agents, who had transferred from California, abused prisoners. This was one of my two big no-no's. First, I demanded total honesty from my employees, and secondly, I forbade any of my agents to abuse their authority. I cannot abide people abusing others because they happen to be in a position of power and control. I'm sure my childhood experience had a lot to do with my perspective on this subject. This particular agent violated both rules. He abused a young man he had in custody and then he lied to me about it. I fired him the next day.

The other guy I fired for being a smart-ass. I was the ARD in Houston and inherited this jerk. He was in charge of Special Investigations. Everyone above him and below him hated the arrogant bastard. The first time he smarted off to me, I let it slide. The second time, about a week later, I told him this: "If you ever talk to me like that again, I will fire your egotistical ass."

I guess he didn't believe me, because about three weeks later he had an impertinence recurrence. This time, I told him this: "Go pack your things. Then take your overbearing, egotistical ass and get the hell out of Dodge (in this case, Dodge being the Houston Regional Office of Investigations), because you, and the horse you rode in on, are totally fucking fired." He seemed shocked. He underestimated me. Which is the point in my little digression. People have often underestimated me. People like Luther Axelrod.

Luther's next move finally resulted in my intervention into this big fiasco.

He said in a sweetly sarcastic voice, "Ahn-hey-leeta, *por favor*, bring another round of Bud Lights for me and my *compadres*, Chango, Doobie, and *mi compadre nuevo*, Daniel."

"We have worked up such a thirst talking to your *novio*," Luther said, placing his hand on Daniel's shoulder. Daniel flinched and laughed nervously. Angelita flinched, but kept her composure. She was quite brave for a fourteen-year-old girl. She brought the three beers and set them in front of the corrupt threesome. She was not about to bring a beer for Daniel.

Then it happened: Luther struck — like a snake. He grabbed Little Angel by the arm and jerked her into his lap. His ruddy complexion instantly turned crimson. His voice started low and started to climb, "I told you to bring Bud Lights for all of my friends. You forgot one for Danny Boy."

Angelita began to struggle. Her struggle was in vain. Luther was a very strong, and obviously deranged man. "Listen up, you little cunt, and learn this: always, always do what I tell you. I don't want to hurt you, so don't ever give me a fucking reason to. Understand?"

When I saw Luther grab Angelita, my movement was automatic. My reflexes were, at once, surprisingly quick and amazingly stealthy. That is, I was surprised and amazed, but not until later. Showtime! In the span it took Luther to get to the word "understand," I had crossed the twenty feet between us and was grabbing him hard around the neck. It happened so fast, no one, especially Luther, saw it coming. They were too busy watching Angelita squirm. I whispered in Luther's amoral ear, "Let the child go. Now."

He croaked back, "Why should I?"

I countered as quietly as possible, "Because, I will break your fucking neck if you don't."

Luther relaxed his grip and Angelita wriggled free. I felt an ape-like paw grab my arm, but I had anticipated this. Before Chango could say, "Listen, motherfu..." I had pulled my S&W Model 59 from under my jacket with my right hand, turned instantly, still holding Luther by the neck, and inserted my weapon, sideways, into Chango's mouth. I heard teeth chipping and saw a splatter of Chango-blood fly. He was still seated and still trying to talk. But his words came out as, "Mm gnnn glll ooo, ummmfffrr." Too late, Chango.

With a clockwise snap of my wrist, the gun was upright in Jacinto Ocala's mouth. We could all hear teeth grinding and cracking. He had a mouth full of S&W sandwich. Chango shut the fuck up. Dwayne DuBois had been watching all of this with eyes wide open and mouth wide closed. Good move on his part. From behind the bar, Little Angel asked, "Should I call the Sheriff, Jaime?" I said no. For several reasons. Not the least being that I did not have a permit to carry a handgun. But having carried one for practically all of my adult life, I wasn't planning to stop now. I also knew nothing would happen to these three assholes. They wouldn't spend more than an hour in jail. And they surely would never be convicted of a crime. But I might be.

I said to Angelita, "Take Daniel and your grand-mother and go home. Leave me the key, I'll lock up. Do it now." And she did.

When it was just Los Diablos and me left in Reynaldo's, I took the gun out of Chango's bloody mouth, let go of Luther's unholy neck and stepped back two paces. I suggested, strongly, that the three amigos remain very still. Then I explained to them: "If you ever lay a hand on the girl, the old lady, or Daniel, I will hunt you down like the low-life, spineless, moth-erfuckers you are and put a hole in each one of your shit-filled skulls. And, I'll like it. A lot. Now, get the fuck out of Dos Cruces."

Dwayne elected not to make eye contact, but Chango and Luther glared at me. Then Luther smiled his sadistic smile and the hair on the back of my neck stood at attention. Los Diablos didn't notice. They just got up and left. And I stood there feeling like I had just played a part in an old, and not particularly good, western movie.

Of course, I knew there would be repercussions. I just didn't know in what form or when it would come. I found out, three nights later, when bullets came whistling through the outside bedroom wall at about 3 A.M. Fortunately, the three stooges didn't know I slept on my trusty old couch in my tiny living room. By the time I got off the floor and looked out the back door, they, and the horse they rode in on, were gone.

I didn't bother to report the incident to the authori-ties in Catarino. And in true Dos Cruces fashion, no one asked me anything about it. Ever. Privacy is highly regarded in this little village. Even Angelita, other than asking me if I was okay the next morning, never said another word about the incident at Reynaldo's. I guess she figured that if she didn't talk about it, it didn't happen. I was more than willing to play that game. I just wanted to be left alone. I never did get over the vague, uneasy feeling that I had not seen the last of Luther Axelrod. But that uneasiness found its way into the basement of my memory bank. And that basement was soon flooded with more guilt, grief, and Miller Lite. So much so that I forgot all about Los Diablos.

Chapter 6

The Killing of Little Angel

A ritual evolved at St. Charles Place on Saturday mornings. I would wake up at 6:00 and start breakfast — a six-pack of Miller Lite. At 6:55, Daniel would knock on the back door. When I answered the door, he would excitedly move his arms back and forth, as if mowing, and say, *"javelinas allí, javelinas allí,"* and then point at my Lilliputian plot, laughing all the while. I would get my dad's old lawnmower out of the shed and start it for Daniel. Fifteen minutes later, the lawnmower would stop. Daniel would take it back to the shed and return to the back door. Again he would knock. I would come to the door and say, *"Entre, mi amigo."* Daniel would smile a very big smile and come into my very small kitchen.

I would have his favorite cereal, Fruit Loops, and a ten-dollar bill waiting for him on the old wooden kitchen table. I would pull out his chair and he would sit down. I would pour the milk on his cereal and bring him a glass of orange juice. Then I would sit across the little table from him and continue my libatious breakfast. Daniel would just eat and grin, eat and grin.

After breakfast, we would adjourn to my cozy living room and watch cartoons, while I continued my aqueous sustenance. The Tasmanian Devil was Daniel's favorite. He would get up from the couch, start spinning around, mumbling and growling, just like Taz. It was uncanny. But Daniel could not bear to stay at my place for more than an hour. Like an abused dog my family once adopted, he craved affection, but too much at one time made him nervous and he would leave to check on his goats. Daniel's laughter would still be ringing in my little house an hour later.

To my sweet amazement, I began to look forward to this little sacrament. And know this: the list of things that I anticipated with any pleasure was quite paltry. I know Daniel, too, looked forward to our get-together because he and his grin showed up every Saturday, like clockwork. Eventually he brought his new one-eyed hound, Taz, our latest companion. I'm not sure where Daniel got him and it really doesn't matter. I treated the pooch like royalty, too. And he actually watched cartoons with Daniel and me. But I won't tell you the dog's favorite show was Scooby-Doo.

Although I thought I'd never be whole again, time in Dos Cruces, which is much slower than time elsewhere, began to work its healing magic on Jamey Maxwell. In spite of my burden of guilt and grief, I started to see small delights in the oddest places. Daniel and Angelita became my substitute children. My surrogate fatherhood skills, however, were terminally deficient.

In a way, it was role reversal. They looked after me, in their own ways, as much as I looked after them. Two years passed. Time was creeping. And creeps were returning to Dos Cruces.

Regarding my relationship with God: when I first moved to Dos Cruces, we weren't speaking, for obvious reasons. He was around, making sure I didn't prematurely end my misery. He needed me. *Bueno.* Maybe I would need Him again, sometime (which I did).

I never hated God for what He did to my family, because I was the one who screwed up. I was the one who begged God to make the deal when I was nine years old. But, I sure didn't appreciate His diligence in regards to punishing me. And I certainly didn't appreciate the fact that my beautiful wife and daughters had to suffer because of my sins. But it's hard to blame God for being God. It's His job. So we muddled through our relationship for three years until things started hopping in Dos Cruces. Then things changed with God and me.

On the morning of Saturday, February 14th, Saint Valentine's Day, six months ago, at approximately 7:45 A.M., my life took another downhill detour. I had been up since 5:30 thinking about Connie, Julie, and Josie — my Valentines. And, of course, I was having my morning refreshment. It was Miller Time. Then came the sirens. First, just one. Then another. Then a third, and a fourth. Although God talks to me now and again, this time I had no warning. But I did have a gut feeling that these sirens were singing to me. I was right. Within thirty minutes my closest neighbor,

Ramón Falcón, knocked on the front door.

Angelita Cavazos' body had been found behind Daniel Galván's hut. In his goat pen. Daniel was still holding her. Her neck had been broken. Her skull was crushed. She may have been raped. Daniel, the goat-boy, Borrego, had been arrested by Sheriff Arlen Buckner for the murder of Angelita Cavazos. Little Angel.

Death's cold, bony finger had been jammed up my ass one more time. And these are the questions I asked God: Okay, God, what did I do this time? And was it so bad that these two innocents had to pay the price? Why do You hate me so? No answer.

I have developed two theories about my relationship with God. Please contemplate them with me. First, I am the only real person on earth. Everyone else is an automaton. If this is the case, I guess you won't be able to contemplate this first theory with me. I am one of God's lab rats. Or maybe one of God's TV shows or off-Broadway (way off-Broadway) plays. There may be millions or billions of these going on throughout the universe. If there is a universe. It could just be a prop. Why else would people that I love suffer for my transgressions?

The only logical answer to this question is theory number two: Los Diablos (Luther Axelrod, Dwayne DuBois, and Jacinto Ocala) were so evil, so destructive to God's plan, that He had to torture me to the point that I would commit the atrocious acts required. He programmed me to become a hard-hearted assassin, a grim reaper, His avenging angel. If this was His game plan, it worked. But wouldn't this mean that the universal battle of good and evil — of God's angelic warriors versus Satan's mercenaries — is so tenuous that it took the martyrdom of one innocent little girl, Angelita Cavazos of Dos fucking Cruces, to tip the scales back to His favor?

I went to Dora Cavazos' house across the railroad tracks and the main highway from St. Charles Place. My purpose was to console her over the loss of her granddaughter. But Dora was holding up much better than I was. Trite, inane condolences were expressed and I went back home, to console myself. And to burrow further into my grief and guilt hole. I had been digging it for the last three years. I fortified it with copious amounts of Miller Lite. The next morning, early, Mrs. Galván, Daniel's mother, came to my house. She was in tears. She spoke almost no English and I've already told you how poor my Spanish is. Mrs. Cavazos was asking me to help Daniel. "*Por favor, Señor Maxwell, Daniel tiene muchos problemas. Tiene mucho* trouble. Daniel no kill Angelita. *Por favor, puede ayudar Daniel? Por favor,* help him." I told her I would. "*Yo ayudo Daniel. No problema, Señora.* Don't worry."

It wasn't really optional. Mrs. Cavazos' request might as well have come directly from You-Know-Who. God had a plan, but at this point, He wasn't sharing the particulars with Jamey Maxwell. Where was I to start? What could I do to help Daniel? I was doing a shitty job just trying to help myself. The rest of the day I spent making coffee and sitting at my kitchen table making notes. Poor Daniel. If I was his best or only hope, *pobrecito!* It had been so long since my mind had really functioned. Anguish, anger, guilt, and grief had been my mantra for two and one-half years. It seemed like an eternity. Surprisingly, by nightfall, I had one or two modest ideas. And, even more surprisingly, I had not had a beer since Mrs. Galván had left.

Bright and early on February 16th, I walked over to the Galván compound. I knocked on Mrs. Galván's door and asked, as best I could in Spanish, if I could take a look around Daniel's little house and goat pen. She replied, "*Sí, sí, Señor Maxwell. Bueno. Gracias. Gracias.*" She was very happy to see me. I could see the hope in her eyes. There was very little of that particular commodity in my heart. I hoped against hope that my hope would return. There was still yellow, plastic crime-scene tape around Daniel's shack. I ignored it and lowered my head to enter the front and only door. It was evident that Sheriff Buckner and his boys had gone through everything Daniel had. It couldn't have taken very long. *No tiene mucho.* He doesn't have much.

I strongly suspected Daniel's place had been searched without the inconvenience of obtaining a search warrant. Sheriff Buckner would probably claim it was a consent search. Technically, I'm sure it was. Daniel would consent to almost anything that almost anybody wanted. But Daniel was not competent to make that kind of life-altering decision and Sheriff Buckner knew it. An illegal search would be our team's (so far, our team consisted of me and Daniel) first contention. I would have to get Daniel an attorney and I knew just the aggressive son-of-a-bitch for the job.

What little Daniel had, I inventoried quickly. Any and everything the Sheriff considered possible evidence would have already been bagged, tagged, and taken. All that was left were a few canned goods, an open sack of pinto beans, a couple of pots and pans, a charcoal grill, a few utensils, a picture of Jesus holding a newborn lamb, a homemade wooden table and bench, a small hand-carved crucifix, and a few odds and ends. Except for his goats, Daniel was not into material things. Another reason I liked him.

The southwest corner of the goat pen was also cordoned off with yellow tape. I'm sure the Sheriff's boys had carefully explained to the goats why they should stay away from the crime scene. Into the pen I went, sidestepping goats and their larger droppings, and made my way to the marked-yellow corner. There wasn't a lot to see. On my knees, I made ever smaller concentric circles until I had covered the roughly 12' x 12' area. Close to the heart of the roped-off plot, I found several small spots, just a little darker than the red-brown dirt. With my pocketknife, I raked the flecked dirt into one of the small baggies I had brought for just such a purpose. I had no way of knowing if this was or wasn't important evidence, but it made me feel better just going through the motions.

I would need to interview Mr. and Mrs. Galván and their other children to see if any of them saw or heard anything that might help. I would need a translator, maybe one of the kids, but probably not. From my brief glimpses of Mr. Galván and the Galván children (two or three other sons and one daughter, who all seemed to be in their twenties or thirties) I did not think they would be of much assistance. They looked to be intellectually challenged, if you know what I mean. And in case I haven't mentioned it yet, in my heart, I knew that in no way was Daniel Galván capable of committing such a crime. He was too gentle. So who did it? Whoever it was, he or they were smart. And he or they knew Daniel. He or they may have come close to pulling off a perfect murder by putting Angelita's body in Daniel's goat pen. Because of the brutality of the crime, I had ruled out all women immediately.

Angelita's funeral was held on Tuesday, February 17th, at the Catholic church in Dos Cruces. Father McGinny conducted the service. Father McGinny was from Ireland, but he looked Dos Crucian — dark hair, dark eyes, and he spoke Spanish better than the natives. When I asked Ramón Falcón how long Father McGinny had been in Dos Cruces, he answered: *todo el tiempo*, or "forever." I think maybe the archbishop of this diocese forgot Father McGinny was here or more likely that Dos Cruces even existed. Or maybe Father McGinny had molested a whole gaggle of altar boys and this was his punishment. I've never heard of a priest being somewhere *todo el tiempo*.

Everyone in Dos Cruces was there. Angelita's casket was open and she looked like one of God's angels. I was one of the pallbearers. After Father McGinny's liturgy, we proceeded to the Dos Cruces cemetery (and plastic botanical garden) for the interment of Little Angel. I didn't cry, but my shriveled heart shriveled a little more. Again, I noticed the monuments to angels and children and thought of my Julie and Josie. I needed to visit them soon. And Connie Lee too.

I spent the rest of the day at home, partaking of other spirits and trying to relive, minute by minute, a special day at the beach on Padre Island several years ago. The weather was perfect. The sky was a brilliant blue and cloudless. The water was a transparent green. Even Julie, little miss grumpy herself, was in a good mood. We all worked on constructing a pretty shabby looking sandcastle. Connie, who had already turned forty, looked like a teenager — Julie and Josie's older sister. She was stunning.

God showed me something shortly after the accident that killed my family. And He reminds me of it constantly. Especially when I am doing my best to concentrate on an exceptional day or episode I shared with my three girls. I don't really want to tell you, but again, I don't think it's optional. And, in the event I have not yet shared this with you, God can be exceptionally cruel. Why else would He want to constantly remind me of this: when I was fucking the other woman, my orgasm was at the exact moment my girls were killed. I want all of you to keep that in mind.

On February 18th, I drove to Catarino to visit Daniel in jail. I was dreading it. Daniel should never be locked in a cage and should never be taken away from his goats. Truly, cruel and unusual punishment. Pulling up to the old, non-descript, yellow brick jail next to the old, non-descript, two-story, yellow brick courthouse, I felt queasy. Leaving my gun in the glove box, I reluctantly pulled myself out of the truck and went inside. After explaining who I was, the dispatcher behind the little bulletproof window called the chief jailer. After a pat down, he led me through two locked iron-bar doors, with fifteen or twenty layers of paint — the last being pastel green — and into a small visiting room. After a few minutes, another jailer brought Daniel in. He was wearing an orange jumpsuit, handcuffs, and leg irons.

Daniel looked like a frightened little boy, which he was. The jailer helped him sit in the gray metal chair and then stood by the closed door, watching. Even though Daniel was grinning, I knew he was scared to death. Just as I had supposed, this whole scene depressed the hell out of me. But what could I do, except try to make Daniel feel a little better? I started with a little joke I knew Daniel would like. "*Mi yarde necesita mower,*" I said moving my arms back and forth, "*porque las javelinas allí.*" Daniel laughed, mimicking the mowing motion, in spite of the handcuffs, and repeated, "*javelinas allí, javelinas allí.*"

"*Estás bien, Daniel?*" I asked. He nodded and gave me a forced grin, "*Estoy bien, Señor Jaime.*" Daniel is not an accomplished liar. He was trying to make me feel better. It worked. My next question, "*Qué necesitas?*"

"*Nada, Señor Jaime, nada.*"

Oh Daniel, I thought, I wish I could get you out of here. For the next ten minutes, Daniel and I made silly small talk, mostly about Taz's crazy adventures, in broken English, broken Spanish, and, of course, gestures. I'm sure the jailer thought, "What a couple of maroons!" or something like that. I could have cared a shit less. Daniel felt better. That's all that mattered.

On my way out, I asked to speak with Sheriff Buckner. Not in. Gone to San Antonio on business. Be back tomorrow. So, back to Dos Cruces I went. I resisted the temptation to stop for a six-pack. I needed to stay focused on Daniel's case. A little sacrifice never hurt anybody, right? Actually, it was a pretty big sacrifice. *Bueno*.

Startled and sitting upright, that's how I awoke Thursday morning. It was 4:30. Something had happened. Was it in my dream? Surprisingly, I have had only a few nightmares in the last three years. At least that I have remembered. No, I heard something. Pulling my jeans on in the dark, I shuffled to the front door and pulled it open. Something on the porch. What was it? An unidentified frigging object. Carefully, so as not to knock it off my tiny deck, I opened the screen door just enough to get my hand on this little surprise. Gingerly, I hauled it inside. It was a green ceramic fish container, complete with lid. "What the fuck?" I murmured.

Retreating to the kitchen, I turned the light on and cursorily examined the ceramic *chingadera* (little fucking thing). I said to myself, "This is fishy," and groaned internally at my pathetic pun. I sat the strange gift down and then it hit me. This is like one of the offerings that showed up after my dad's funeral, and again when I first moved to Dos Cruces. Miller Lite. That's what I needed, but I settled for making coffee instead. While the coffee was brewing, I took a quick shower and put on jeans and my holiest tee shirt — my thinking clothes. Back in the kitchen, I poured myself a cup and sat down at the table. Lifting the lid, I immediately saw a small piece of crumpled paper. I opened it. Handwritten, almost illegibly, was this: "I SOM TAUW." Weird, but just about par for the dusty course in Dos Cruces, Texas.

It hit me half way through my second cup of coffee: I had seen this handwriting before. Of course. The sign hanging on the gate in front of the sister's house. Curiouser and curiouser. What did that sign say? I couldn't remember exactly. No problema. Only three Dos Cruces blocks down the street. When daylight comes, I thought, a morning stroll is in order. Daylight did come and I did stroll down to old half-man Dochler's place. The homemade sign on the fenceless gate read "SAEK TAU GOKU." It was definitely written by the same author as the cryptic note in the ceramic fish. What did I make of this? Not much at the time. But as time progressed, more mysterious morning gifts at St. Charles Place would help elucidate. In the meantime, I had other carp to cook.

Back at *mi casa pequeña*, I was calling my old friend, James Boyer, ex-United States Attorney and currently in private practice. We had met in El Paso when I was a Customs Agent and he was an Assistant U.S. Attorney. He and I worked on several cases together, which turned out to be successful prosecutions. We learned to trust each other, which was not always the case with agents and prosecutors. He was transferred to Houston about a year after I was.

We worked together for years and moved up our respective ranks. He eventually became the U.S. Attorney in Houston (Eastern District of Texas) and I became Assistant Regional Director of Investigations of the U.S. Customs Service. We were good friends at work and occasionally on a social basis. James, or Jimmy, as his friends called him, had the reputation of being tough, fair and scrupulously honest. Because he was always impeccably dressed and exuded a rather aristocratic air, the press nicknamed him "Gentleman Jim." They should have seen and heard him behind closed doors. Such language! Even old sailors would blush. But he was always a good friend when I needed him. And I needed him now. His secretary connected me.

"Hey, you old son-of-a-bitch. What the fuck's up?" Gentleman Jim began.

"I love you, too. Good to hear you've cleaned up your act," I retorted, "since going private."

"Come on, Maxwell," Jimmy said, "you know you love it when I talk dirty to you. It really is good to hear from you. I figured you were dead." Sensitivity was not always James Boyer's strong suit.

"No, Jimmy, I'm still alive, if you want to call living in Dos Cruces, Texas, living."

We bantered about for a few more minutes, then I started. "Jimmy, I need your help. There's this kid. He's been arrested for murder. He was caught at his place still holding the victim in his arms. But he didn't do it. He couldn't have. I know you've heard this before, but he's innocent."

For the next thirty minutes or so I went over the entire story of Daniel and Angelita including most of the details. He listened, asked all the right questions, and then asked what I needed him to do. I said, "Jimmy, I want you to represent Daniel. I'll pick up the tab. Will you do it?"

"Of course, you cocksucker. But you already knew that. Here's the deal, I will be down there a week from next Monday. In the meantime, I want you to be my investigator on this case and we'll deduct that from what you owe me. You can pay me the rest in blowjobs."

"It would be my pleasure," I chuckled. "Thanks, Jimmy."

My next challenge, and it would be a challenge, was to interview Daniel's family. Ramón Falcón, my neighbor, agreed to act as translator. My dad had gotten such a kick from repeating his name, which in the Spanish tongue, rhymes: Ra-moan Fal-cone. It was my father's all-time favorite name. Ramón Falcón and I walked over to the Galván complex and knocked on what was left of the old screen door. Mrs. Galván answered. She spoke animatedly to me and Ramón in Spanish, but only Ramón could completely comprehend. I understood bits and pieces. She said Daniel wanted to come home. She did not know how to get him out of jail. The Galván family had never been caught up in the American legal system. To Mrs. Galván, quantum physics would have been no less difficult to understand. Ramón finally got in some words, edgewise, and, eventually, she began to calm down. Ramón explained that we were there to help Daniel, but she, her husband and her children would have to answer some questions first. Mrs. Galván replied, "*Bueno*," and invited us inside.

Apparently, Jamey Maxwell had fallen down a big ol' rabbit hole in Dos Cruces, Texas. But this was no

Wonderland I had stumbled into. Maybe Bizarro World or the Twilight Zone. Inside the Galván house, vertigo and an overpowering stench greeted me. My first thought was: in this universe, Dos Cruces, Texas, is the nexus of reality and surreality. More precisely, the Galván home is the point of intersect. The shack had three rooms and I could see all of them from just inside the front door. Nary a 90-degree angle to be found. Walls and floors linked at acutely obtuse and obtusely acute angles. Dizziness, nausea, and the overwhelming urge to break into hysterical laughter were just a few of the sensations that struck me.

In the Texas Hill Country there is a tourist trap where the main attraction is an anti-gravity house. Everything is an optical illusion. Water appears to run uphill. Walls, floors, and ceilings are all aslant. Tourists sway, stumble, and laugh gleefully until they get their bearings. Then everything looks kind of normal and they leave. The Galván place was both an anti-gravity and anti-reality house, but I had the feeling I could stand here until the end of time and it would never look normal.

The three rooms were a combination living room/bedroom, a combination kitchen/bedroom and a combination bedroom/bedroom. Unlike Daniel's shanty, the main house had a wooden floor. But in some cases, the cracks between the floorboards were wider than the boards themselves. Old rusted tin covered a few of the cracks. Old straw-stuffed mattresses covered some more. From inside the living/bedroom, I had a birds-eye view of the ground and a worms-eye view of the sky. There was no ceiling. Just a roof of additional rusty tin with a plethora of perforations through which dappled sunlight poured. I could see dust fairies dancing in the filtered rays. The see-through walls (interior and exterior were one and the same) were also made out of boards, along with strategically placed cardboard.

The walls were adorned with things like (and I'm not making this up): a picture of the *Virgen de Guadalupe* with various sized tin can lids nailed above and on both sides. Below the Virgin were nine or ten mummified stinging scorpions crucified to the wall and arranged, left to right, by ascending size. A grotesque collage of old magazine pictures, yellowed by smoke, grease, and age, gazed at me from another wall. Marilyn Monroe, Adolf Hitler, Buffalo Bob *con* Howdy Doody, Albert Einstein, an unidentified African tribe *con* topless women, Fritz the Cat, Jesus, and a cast of dozens cried out in a cacophony of silence.

On the floor, in a corner, stood a one-armed Barbie doll. Amputee Barbie was robed in what appeared to be part of an old animal skin. Atop her saucy blond head sat a corona made from tin foil and sticks. In front of her, arranged in a semi-circle, were small animal bones, possibly chicken and rat, some with the flesh and/or feathers still attached. A quaintly bizarre shrine to Saint Barbie. "Oh, Barbie," I thought, "if only Ken could see you now." Randomly strewn across the floors were old goatskins. Old, stinking goatskins, neither cured nor tanned. Apparently, they had been unceremoniously removed from the goats and thrown on the floor to age in place. They were crusty around the edges.

But here's where it really got weird. Sitting erectly in old wooden chairs all around the living room, up against the walls, were the rest of the Galván clan. Daniel's father, three of his brothers, and a sister, were staring straight ahead, oblivious, or so it seemed, to the presence of guests. Intuitively, I sensed they had been sitting like this for a long time. This, I thought, is how they spend their days.

The house had no electricity, therefore no television or radio. Plus, the entire Galván family was, collectively, a few hundred bricks shy of a load. I attempted to make eye contact with one of the brothers sitting directly across from me. Stifling the impulse to collapse in unconstrained cachinnation, I realized Daniel's brother was wall-eyed. Eye contact was not an option.

For some reason, a notion occurred to me: I wonder what the old "alleged" Nazi couple thought about their next door neighbors, the Galváns, in the context of the hypothetical, genetically pure, non-defective Aryan race? Purgatory for some lost souls may look a whole lot like Dos Cruces, Texas.

As an investigator, you never interview witnesses in a group because this has the tendency to change individual reality into group reality. But in the case of the Galván brood, I made an exception because I didn't think it would matter. I wasn't sure how real their reality was to start with. Still standing (since all the chairs in the living room were occupied), I instructed Ramón to ask a series of questions regarding the night before Daniel was found holding Angelita.

With each question, Mrs. Galván, who was also standing, would turn to her husband, who would in turn, turn to one of the sons (never the daughter), and repeat the question. As each question was passed on, I noticed the language changed from Ramón's Spanish into a type of gibberish that was comprised of very little recognizable Spanish, English, or Tex-Mex. The Galván patois did include, however, animated hand and facial gestures. And it sometimes sounded argumentative. As soon as a consensus was reached, the seated Galváns would revert to their previous robot-like posture, staring straight ahead.

After each parlay, Mrs. Galván would answer Ramón in Spanish, most of which I understood. Here was the gist of the thirty-plus minute interrogation: nobody knew nothing about nothing. *No le hace.* Ramón and I thanked the Galván family, and beamed ourselves back to earth.

On the dirt street in front of the Galván place, Ramón Falcón was puffed up like a turkey gobbler in full display. This was the most excitement he had encountered in his sixty-something years in Dos Cruces. This was *Matlock*, *Murder She Wrote*, and *Cops* all rolled into one, with Ramón Falcón as the special guest star. I didn't burst his bubble. I just couldn't. Although terribly disappointed that even Daniel's family couldn't provide an alibi, I pretended that Ramón had single-handedly solved this case. I handed him a ten-dollar bill, which he accepted *sin* hesitation. I thanked him profusely for his inestimable assistance.

"*Gracias, Ramón. Usted es un detectivo bueno.*"

"De nada, Señor Maxwell, me gusta mucho mi trabajo con usted!" He was one happy Dos Crucian.

My next chore, which I was looking forward to about as much as a case of the clap (which, by the way, I've never had), was to interview *los alemanes*, the alleged Dos Cruces Chapter of the Adolf Hitler Fan Club. I decided to get it over with. After bidding Ramón adieu at the Galváns' front gate, I walked next door.

The old German couple's house, I noticed, was actually closer to Daniel's shack than his parents' shack was. No more than a hundred feet away, but partially blocked by a few old salt cedars on the Galván side of the fence. Close enough to have heard anything unusual, or should I say, out of the ordinary — you know what I mean.

As I sauntered slowly, admiring the newest coat of paint on their picket fence, I noticed something germane in the Germans' yard. A dog. Want to guess what kind? You're right, a German Shepherd. The good news was the dog was chained. The bad news was I couldn't tell how long the chain was. Also, I would have to revisit the Galván family, along with ace detective Ramón Falcón, to ask specifically if they had heard *los alemanes'* dog barking that night. I've learned that in Dos Cruces, Texas, you have to be specific.

When I reached the front gleaming white picket gate, I discovered there was a lock on it. The gate was no more than three feet in height. Being six feet tall, I could have easily stepped over it. But between the locked gate and the German Shepherd, I intuited that the old German couple was trying to make a state-ment. Such as: *Achtung!* Keep Out! Survivors Will Be Tortured! What scared me the most was the fact that the German Shepherd never barked, growled, or even whimpered. The strong, silent type I guess. So, I stood at the front gate and shouted, "Is anybody home?"

It sounded really lame, since I already knew the answer. A white curtain on the window next to the immaculately painted front door moved just a tad. I could see two fingers and an eyeball. Then the curtain was still. I detected a look of silent disgust on the watchdog's face. "Hey buddy, the feeling's mutual," I thought to myself, hoping the mutt wasn't a mind reader. This interview would have to be postponed pending a court order and, hopefully, within the proximity of a deputy sheriff or two.

Thus far, I was 0 for 2. Batting .000. Nothing accom-plished. No help to Daniel. Once I had been a pretty damn good investigator. Obviously, that was in another life, in a galaxy far, far away. I needed to get all of my shit in one basket and all of my turds in a row. But first, I needed a beer. So I ambled home to St. Charles Place. Popping open a Miller Lite, I sat down at the kitchen table with a Big Chief tablet, one of my dad's old leftovers.

I scribbled down a few notes regarding my fruitless Galván interview and attempted Germanic interview. Mostly just to keep busy until the beer-induced enlightenment kicked in. It took about three M-Ls to get there. I was determined however to limit my brew intake to a six-pack or less a day. I really had cut down and I was pretty damn proud of myself for it. Here was my revised game plan: (1) drive to Catarino, and (2) talk to Sheriff Arlen Buckner.

Chapter 7

Sheriff Arlen Buckner

Sheriff Arlen T. Buckner strolled into his office and I rose to meet him. He was different than I had imagined him. Less rednecked. More polished and professional. A yuppie cowboy. Buckner was between forty-five and fifty years old. About my age. Slender. About my height. His mustache was neatly trimmed. Like mine. He wore an expensive gray felt Stetson with a George Strait crease, a brown tweed sports coat over a starched khaki shirt, and severely starched and dangerously creased blue jeans. If you weren't careful, you could cut yourself on them. Sheriff Arlen Buckner himself had a sharp edge, softened only by a pair of round wire frame glasses and a boyish smile that could melt an eighty-year-old whore's heart.

Sheriff Buckner stuck out his hand, smiled, and said sardonically, "Mr. Maxwell, it's always nice having a new visitor to my humble chambers. To what do I owe this pleasure?" I could see why he had been in office for eighteen years. Even when being patronizing, he was charming. The locals had to love this guy. Most of his wry wit was probably wasted in Losoya County, but I'm sure his charisma had a bewitching influence on even the most cynical of his citizens. Pulling the wool over constituents' eyes was the proverbial piece of cake, I'm sure, for Sheriff Arlen T. Buckner.

"Sheriff Buckner," I began and was immediately interrupted.

"Please call me Arlen. That's what my friends call me. Among other things," he chuckled.

"Arlen," I continued, "I'd like to talk to you about Daniel Galván."

"You mean our notorious, and only murderer, in the recent history of Losoya County. What would you like to know about the lad?" Buckner inquired.

"Well, several things. And there's a few things I would like to share with you about Daniel," I answered.

"Are you a friend of his?" the Sheriff smiled sardonically, eyebrows arching. He was being cautiously facetious.

"Actually, yes I am," I said, momentarily embarrassed and somewhat surprised that I had never really thought of Daniel in that way. But he was. He definitely was. A good friend.

Sheriff Arlen Buckner was perplexed, but only for an instant. He was a very astute observer of the human animal and I could tell the good Sheriff was seldom caught off guard. Once he saw I was serious, he transformed accordingly. The guy was amazing.

What a chameleon. What a politician.

"Mr. Maxwell," he started and this time I interrupted. "Call me Jamey. That's what my friend calls me. I only have one, Daniel. Actually, he calls me Señor Jaime, but you can just call me Jamey."

I wasn't sure why I was baiting Sheriff Buckner. Probably because of this: when you get to the point in life where you don't care if you live or die, it's a special kind of freedom. And you don't much give a javelina's ass about what other people think. Particularly people who are, let's say, less than humble.

"Okay Jamey," Sheriff Buckner said, "let me explain something to you. This might help. Daniel Galván was caught in his goat pen, holding Angelita Cavazos in his arms. Her neck was broken. Her skull was crushed. He had her blood all over him. She had been raped vaginally and anally. (Flinching, hopefully not too noticeably, I thought, Angelita, *pobrecita*.) He willingly made an oral confession. Actually, several oral confessions. To me, to the Texas Rangers, and to the District Attorney's investigator. Then he signed a written confession.

"This was a disgustingly brutal crime, Mr. Maxwell. So much so that Judge Durán has ordered Mr. Galván held without bond. Now, this is my first murder case and I don't profess to being Sherlock Holmes or even Sheriff Andy Taylor. But this appears to be a pretty cut-and-dried case, wouldn't you say?" His voice never rose, but his eyes betrayed his anger. Sheriff Arlen Buckner was a man who did not like wearing his emotions on his starched khaki sleeves.

This was the first I had heard about the rape accusation. My first thought was: poor Angelita, you did not deserve any of this. Then, poor Daniel, it's getting worse. Suddenly, though, it came to me: DNA testing. Daniel's innocence could be proven, definitively. I decided to give Sheriff Buckner a short pause to collect himself.

Then I started, "Sheriff Buckner, can I ask you a couple of questions?" I tried to sound as respectful as possible.

"Mr. Maxwell, you can ask me anything you like. And, I'll do my best to give you a straight answer. But you may not like what you hear."

"I'll take my chances," I said and immediately thought, oops, here I go again. "Are you aware that Daniel Galván has the mind of a five-year-old child?" I asked.

Buckner shot back, "Even five-year-olds know that killing somebody is wrong. And, besides, he has the body and the urges of a thirty-five year old man."

Having started with my least offensive question, I followed it up with, "Did Daniel have an attorney present when he made his confession?"

"Your boy, Daniel, elected not to have legal counsel present and signed a waiver to that effect," the honorable Sheriff curtly replied.

"Could I see a copy of his confession?" I inquired, already knowing the answer.

"Are you an attorney, Mr. Maxwell? And even if you are, I have seen no documentation indicating that Daniel Galván has chosen you to act in that capacity. In fact, Judge Durán has already assigned a court appointed attorney, Mr. Edgar Wright, since your friend appears to be unable to afford one."

Sheriff Arlen Buckner was starting to enjoy this immensely. He was also starting to underestimate me. I hate it when that happens.

My last question, and I had saved the best for last, was this: "Since Daniel speaks very little English, or Spanish for that matter, and I'm quite sure he can't read or write, just how was he able to confess, apparently in sordid detail, to such a heinous crime?"

Sheriff Buckner's grinned and said, "We have our ways of communicating with Daniel Galván, Mr. Maxwell, we have our ways. Now, I don't want to sound rude, but I have other constituents to try to make happy. It's been my pleasure to make your acquaintance. Hopefully, we can get together in the near future."

As I stood to leave, the honorable Sheriff Arlen T. Buckner asked, "Mr. Maxwell, where, exactly, were you on the evening of February 13th and the early morning of February 14th of this year?" Clearly, Sheriff Buckner was trying to intimidate me.

"In Dos Cruces, Texas, snuggled in my bed," I replied too cheerfully. Then I added, "And no, there is no one who can corroborate this."

"On more thing, Mr. Maxwell," Buckner continued, "I'm sure you're aware that in Dos Cruces, Daniel Galván is known as *el chingador de cabras*, 'the goat fucker.'"

"Yes," I replied, "and the *batos* who call him that are the same ones who refer to you as 'that cocksucking sheriff'. Now, I've known Daniel for three years and have yet to see him fucking a goat. I've only known you for a few minutes, Sheriff Buckner, but I'm willing to give you the benefit of the doubt."

I knew I had gone over the edge. But, by this point, it didn't really matter. The good Sheriff and I were never going to be drinking buddies. Buckner dropped his head and appeared to be looking at some papers on his desk. Then he slowly looked up with his best election-winning grin and said, "Point well taken, Mr. Maxwell."

Some people, like Daniel and me, use our smiles as defense mechanisms. Sheriff Arlen Buckner uses his smile as a political tool to win people over or, failing that, to slice and dice them down to a trifle. Quite effective. The honorable Sheriff then added, "Now, Mr. Maxwell, please get the fuck out of my office." And I did.

Back in Dos Cruces, I called Jimmy Boyer and asked him about the possibility of a bond reduction hearing. Jimmy said, "I'm working on it even as you speak. But you know, Maxwell, the bond will still be fucking exorbitant. No less than $500,000, probably $1,000,000. I'm known more for my large dick than for my mathematical genius, but I figure 10 percent would come out to be $100,000, if he's lucky $50,000. From what you've told me, your friend, Daniel, probably couldn't post a fifty fucking dollar bond. Am I missing something?"

"Yeah," I said, "the fact that I'm going to put up the money. And, before you ask, yes, I am out of my fucking mind."

"Hey, this is your rodeo, Maxwell, I'm just along

for the ride. But, I've got to tell you, you're putting your balls on the chopping block. And as I recall, they're not that big. But they are all you have."

I replied, "*No problema*, I don't have much use for 'em anymore." When I asked Jimmy about DNA testing he said he would try to get the court to order it.

"But, if the court won't do it, you'll have to fork up the moola yourself, Jamey. It's real fucking expensive and unlike me, they won't let you pay for it in blowjobs."

I said, "*Yo comprendo.* And, by the way Jimmy, nobody uses the word 'moola' anymore."

He laughed, said, "fuck you, Maxwell," and hung up. I felt better. Probably shouldn't have.

Grief. Let's talk about it. There is such a thing as good grief, I think. Good grief lets you live your life on your own terms. None of the customary rules apply. No pressure. People treat you as they might a leper. An untouchable to be pitied. You make them uncomfortable. You embarrass them. They don't know the words to say, because there aren't any.

Now, many folks would consider this punishment. But for one who has experienced suffering and isolation at an early age, and has anticipated horrible tidings most of his life, based on a covenant with God, grief can be a sanctuary. All the pressure is off. Eccentricities that were always attendant are at once obvious and forgiven. Human beings, especially friends and family, are happy to absolve you of all sins, write them off to anguish and suffering, particularly if they can do it from a distance. As long as they don't have to say those hollow, meaningless words.

And don't get too close to them — your bad fortune might be contagious. You can get used to grief, start liking it, look forward to it. Snuggle down into your safe and secure, self-serving, comforter of sorrow. It's so cozy. No one can touch you there. They don't even want to.

Sitting at the little table in the little kitchen of my little house, I figured I had made a little progress (very little) on my crusade to save Daniel, the goatboy, from a life of indoor plumbing, central heating and air conditioning, tile floors, and three square meals a day — but without goats. I had come up with doodly squat. Plus, this: whoever killed (and raped, but I don't want to think about that) Little Angel, knew Daniel. They more than likely knew Daniel's relationship with Angelita. At this point, I figured it was a local *bato*, between the age of fifteen and forty-five, acting alone. Someone who had thought about it, planned it, premeditated it, and probably for a while. He was a strong, extremely vicious, socio/psycho-path. And extremely clever. He might just have committed the perfect crime.

But I didn't really think so. In fact, God was already murmuring in my ear, in my voice as usual, that this case would be solved. God apparently had decided to play the part of Sergeant Joe Friday. That would make me Officer Bill Gannon, I suppose. Just the facts, ma'am. Just the facts.

On Saturday, February 21st, at 4:30 A.M., I awoke suddenly, *otra vez*. This time I knew what it was. I went straight to the front door, opened it, and saw the small benefaction on the porch. A rough-carved wooden bowl with no lid. It contained what looked like a round stone. I brought the offering inside. The stone-like object turned out to be an old paperweight. Under it was another message. This time it read, in the same, nearly indecipherable, scrawl: "TARUU OB TAUW." Another love note from the sisters? Probably. But with my luck, it was from the ugly one. Quaintly interesting. That's how the little gifts *con* notes seemed.

At this time I had no reason to see any correlation with Angelita's murder. I was not, as yet, receiving communiqués on that frequency. So I sat my little *objets de yunke* aside for the time being. After all, I had other gaspergou to grill. The remainder of my weekend was quiet, uneventful. Only consumed a six-pack, total. Three beers a day average. Getting to be a regular teetotaler. Pretty proud of myself. What a guy! *Qué hombre!* Too bad there was only myself to be proud of me.

Guilt. Let's talk about it. Whereas grief can be a warm, feathery comforter filled with down of sorrow, a perverse solace; guilt is a cold, stainless steel autopsy table. And each day, at some point, you awaken to find yourself laid out under a glaring light. Guess who is required to perform the postmortem? You are correct, sir. You are compelled to do it yourself.

On the good days, a gleaming, sharpened scalpel is at your disposal. Carefully you make the incision, cautiously poke and prod, and seeing nothing amiss, sew yourself back up using fine surgical thread. Then come the bad days. An old rusty-bladed butcher knife, dull and jagged, is the only instrument at hand. And let me assure you, the examination is not optional. It must be performed.

So you carelessly rip yourself open, leaving a gaping wound with raggedy edges. Staring inside, all you can see is layer upon layer of black, rotted tissue, in the varying stages of ossification. And forgetting that you are no longer among the living, you panic and begin to stab and slash at the decaying guilt meat. You want so much to rid yourself of it — to rip it out. You want to scream. But to whom? And about what? To God? About your sins? Do you really think He wants to hear that crap? Save your breath.

And in an endless cycle of abhorrence, what you tear out is instantly replaced by more putrid, petrifying condemnation. Enough. Please, enough. Using strips of rotten, stinking goat hide, you suture yourself back up. And await tomorrow with dread.

Chapter 8

Marisol of Dos Cruces

Assuming that all inhabitants of Earth are real — and this is just an assumption as far as I'm concerned — there are certain people who are preternaturally drawn towards each other. Often for no perceptible reason. And I'm not necessarily talking about love, lust, neediness, etcetera.

Sometimes it just clicks and can be simultaneously scary and nice. This is how it was between Marisol Cortinas, District Attorney for the 185th District of Texas, and Jamey Maxwell, chief reprobate of Dos Cruces, Texas.

Long ago, as a federal agent, I learned never to make appointments with people from whom you are trying to extract information. Don't give them time to prepare. To make up bullshit stories. Surprise can be a wonderful ally or a worthy adversary, depending upon which side you're on. I had done this with Sheriff Arlen T. Buckner and I was going to do it with

D.A. Marisol Cortinas.

So, once again I hopped in my trusty Chevy S-10 truckette, and headed for Catarino for a surprise visit. I wanted to see if I could piss her off as much as I was able to piss off the good sheriff. The surprise visit turned out to be a big surprise to me.

I stopped at a small mom-and-pop convenience store on the south side of Catarino. I grabbed a Dr. Pepper and the local weekly newsrag, the *Catarino Bulletin*. Of course, the murder (the rape wasn't mentioned) of Angelita Cavazos was the lead story and pretty much the entire front page. Sheriff Arlen T. Buckner had arrested the killer, Daniel Galván, and assured the citizens of Losoya County that justice would be swift.

Although he didn't mention in the interview that he was up for re-election in May, an ad on the second page did. "Re-elect Sheriff Arlen T. Buckner. He puts criminals where they belong. Behind bars." This slogan was accompanied by a picture of a man behind bars. That man just happened to be Daniel Galván. I suddenly realized two things: (1) how effective this picture would be in getting Sheriff Arlen T. Buckner re-elected; and (2) how much I despised him for it.

Back at the unostentatious Losoya County Courthouse, I climbed the generic stairway to the generic offices of the District Attorney. The generic receptionist offered me a generic chair while waiting for D.A. Cortinas. I wasn't even sure she would see me, but when she stepped into the reception area all thoughts of the generic evaporated. Certain people in this world pulsate light waves from a spectrum only a privileged few can see. Marisol Cortinas emitted rays of radiance and anger, kindness and fury, mistrust and hopefulness. She was at war within herself, battles constantly raging. It was killing her. In a burst of comprehension, I could see all of this in her eyes. Very strange.

She was also beautiful, although she didn't care. Neither did I, Jamey Maxwell, sex zombie. But her kinetic energy seemed to be recharging a cell or two of my well-nigh dead cosmic battery.

"What can I do for you Mr. Maxwell?" she said, at once blunt and earnest. Marisol Cortinas was a shade over five feet tall, thick black hair pulled back in a bun, probing dark brown eyes, perfectly proportioned, flawless olive skin, impeccably dressed, and not the hint of a smile. She was in full body (and soul) armor. "Would it be possible to discuss the Daniel Galván case with you? I just need a few minutes of your time," I said, a little too sincerely.

"Of course," she replied. "Follow me." And I did.

Marisol's office was sanitarily professional, with minimal, but tasteful, decorations. She tried hard not to provide clues to her vulnerabilities. Fear was not the reason for her elaborate internal and external defenses. My perception was she just didn't like the human race all that much. Imagine that. What's not to like?

Marisol Cortinas was not into perfunctory banter, which I appreciated, so I got straight to the point. "Daniel Galván is innocent," I declared. "I know him. He is not capable of committing this crime."

Ms. Cortinas gazed intently into my eyes. She was

sizing me up, looking for the angle. When she had found none, she stated, "I know Daniel Galván. I grew up with him."

I tried to hide my surprise, but was not successful. She had wrested the initiative from me, but it didn't matter. No hidden agenda here. I sat there for a few seconds, gathering my scattered thoughts.

Before I could speak, she continued. "I was raised in Dos Cruces, Mr. Maxwell." I didn't bother to say, just call me Jamey. I was a mister to her. "Daniel was maybe four or five years older than me. I'm not sure exactly, since none of the Galván kids attended school." How could that be, I wondered, with truancy laws and such. Then I remembered: we're talking about Dos Cruces, Texas.

Her voice was firm, soft, and not just a little sexy (from a clinical point of view, that is). I was allowing myself to be enchanted, which was, of course, ridiculous. Finally, I spoke up, "I didn't realize you were from Dos Cruces, Ms. Cortinas. How well did you know Daniel?"

She betrayed just the hint of a smile and replied, "Well, Mr. Maxwell, being from Dos Cruces yourself, you should know how a small town works. Especially that small town." I was very surprised to learn that she knew about me. Also, her bitterness toward Dos Cruces did not go unnoticed. "Everyone knows everything about everyone."

"How did you know I'm from Dos Cruces?" I chuckled.

And she said, with just the right amount of drollery, "Would you believe your newfound friend, Sheriff

Buckner, told me? He also warned me to be very vigilant if I crossed your path. Sheriff Buckner thinks you're a dangerous man, Mr. Maxwell. Are you?"

"What do you think Ms. Cortinas? Do I look dangerous to you?" I grinningly asked.

"I can't tell yet," she said, then added, "Besides, I'm not good at reading people." This was a lie, but not a malicious one. She was an expert.

Outwardly attempting to project composure, since my insides were churning with obsolete emotions, I asked, "Do you believe Daniel is guilty?"

Marisol was momentarily caught off guard, as if she had never considered this question. She flashed a pensive pout and answered, "Daniel was caught red-handed, literally speaking. The evidence I have seen is devastating. It's unlike any case I have ever been involved in. So, to be perfectly honest, I really have not considered the possibility of his innocence. Mr. Maxwell, I have not seen or spoken with Daniel for at least fourteen years. When I lived in Dos Cruces, I never felt threatened by him in any way. He had the mind and disposition of a child. Always smiling and pleasant. But I have seen things, cruelties, in this line of work that I never believed were possible. I am no longer a naïve person and I can't even remember when that change occurred. Yes, at this point, I believe Daniel is guilty. I wish it were not the case. Do you have proof to the contrary, Mr. Maxwell?"

"Not yet," I mumbled, as much to myself as to her, "not yet."

I was beginning to wonder why I had come in the first place. Marisol Cortinas was probably wondering the same thing. I related my theory that it had to be someone who knew both Angelita and Daniel, as well as their connection. I profiled the hypothetical killer for her. Trying her best not to be patronizing, Marisol said what I had already begun to believe. If somebody else committed this crime, they might well have devised a near-perfect murder scheme.

We talked about the possibility of DNA testing. She was straightforward on this matter, "Unless you or someone else can produce another legitimate suspect, the cost of testing, from the state's and county's point of view, is unwarranted. Even if the DNA test was not a match for Daniel, and even if his confession is thrown out, the other evidence is overwhelming."

I told her that I had retained an attorney on Daniel's behalf and we intended to pursue every avenue available, including paying for DNA tests, to prove his innocence.

"I truly admire what you are doing for Daniel, Mr. Maxwell. And, unlike Sheriff Buckner, I'm not going to question your motives. But I want you to consider something as objectively as possible," Ms. Cortinas said with surprising sincerity.

"What's that?" I asked.

She began, "You have seen how Daniel has lived his life. The depressing conditions. The squalor. I realize this is no fault of his parents. The Galván family, all of them, as I'm sure you're aware, are mentally handicapped. They would not be allowed to live like this anywhere in this country, except Dos Cruces, Texas. Due to his diminished mental capacity, Daniel will not be sent to prison. Have you considered the worst that will happen to Daniel is being committed to a mental institution for the rest of his life? He would be clean, well fed. He could watch television. Learn to make new friends. Live a decent life. He doesn't see things on the same scale as you and I. Have you thought of any of this, Mr. Maxwell?"

I answered her this way: "Yes, actually I have Ms. Cortinas, Marisol, and I asked myself one question that ruined the whole scenario."

"And what is that?" she asked, and I could tell she really wanted to know.

I grinned and said, "Would they let him keep his goats there?"

Marisol Cortinas smiled the most beautiful smile, one that had probably not been seen in years, and Jamey Maxwell's long frozen heart began to thaw.

On my way back to Dos Cruces, apparitions began to play hide-and-seek inside Jamey Maxwell's haunted-house memory: little girls, hearts pure and clothes filthy, with dreamy, introspective smiles, making mud pies; a beautiful wife wearing only her husband's T-shirt and a come-hither look; a young waitress full of life and desperation, yet being gentle with her favorite customer; a delicate young man surrounded by winged goats; a dark-haired beauty, serious and seductive, with the mythical voice of a siren. Terminal melancholia.

I stopped at the mom-and-pop store just south of Catarino *una vez más*. But no Dr. Pepper this time. Oh no, that wasn't going to cut the fucking mustard. This situation called for Miller Lite. A twelve-pack. I wasn't falling off the wagon. I was taking a magnificent,

Olympic-caliber swan dive. And you know what? I didn't give a shit. Only eight left when I got back to St. Charles Place. Fuck supper. Polished off M-Ls. Crashed on disgusting, but not entirely uncomfortable, sofa. Slept late. 6:10 A.M. Eerie feeling should check front porch. Feeling accurate. New offering. Cast iron piggy bank. Note inside. Dos Cruces weird place.

This time the note read: "LOS DIABLOS." It was the same handwriting as before, but this time I didn't need an interpreter. *Los Diablos*. "The Devils." Dos Cruces weird place. Jamey Maxwell go crazy.

Miller Lite was sorely needed, but someone had consumed it all. Probably my evil twin. So I made some coffee, extra strong. Something a real man would drink. But until one came along, I would have a cup or two myself. A premonition presented itself in the form of a question. God was playing the Mysterious One again. Do these cryptic notes have something to do with the rape and murder of Angelita Cavazos? "Goddamnit, why can't You just give me a straight answer? Why do You have to make everything a fucking riddle?"

God didn't say anything. Maybe I hurt His feelings. But after a few minutes, the answer came. The answer was: maybe. Whooptie-fucking-do. Sometimes God really pisses me off. But then again, I think He likes it. A lot.

To be perfectly honest, I didn't feel like being a detective today. Maybe tomorrow. My body, mind, and soul (what little of that corrupt ephemeron remained) were exhausted. Totally whacked. Please

God, cut me some slack. *Por favor?*

Surprisingly, however, the pounding in my brain had managed to knock loose a capital idea. Actually, it was a shitty idea, but I liked it anyway. I would call Marisol Cortinas with the pretext of sharing some more interesting conspiracy theories...and ask her out for lunch. At 8:30 A.M., I called the District Attorney's office and was greeted by the generic receptionist with a slightly annoying voice. I identified myself and asked to speak with Ms. Cortinas. At this point, I was having second, third, and fourth thoughts about my plan to ask a District Attorney out to lunch. I think it's called sobering up. Anyway, I figured she just wouldn't answer the phone. Again, fucked figuring.

"Hello, Mr. Maxwell. What can I do for you?" the voice jarred me to my senses. What a straight line, I thought.

"Well, Ms. Cortinas...Marisol, I...I've been thinking about Angelita and...I...I have some new ideas...a theory...that I would like to run by you. And...I...I was wondering if you...might be free to...to go to...lunch, today...to...to discuss ...them...or it," I stammered. What a maroon!

"Mr. Maxwell, are you asking me out on a date?" Marisol inquired. This caught me completely off guard. She could probably feel me blushing over the phone line. I couldn't tell if she was cross-examining me or just kidding. Maybe both.

"N...n...no...no. I just thought if you weren't too b...busy...I'm s...sorry...I shouldn't have called...b...bad idea." Jesus Christ, I was actually stuttering. What a fucking maroon!

"Actually, I think it's a fine idea," said Ms. Cortinas in a voice containing just a hint of a flirt. I think. "But could we make it supper instead? I have a meeting in Laredo this afternoon. Would you be able to meet me at Serrano's at Sol del Rio Mall at about 6:00? I know it's a bit of a drive for you, but I would love to hear your new theory. I've got a couple of things to bounce off you." Was this another straight line? Probably not.

I had progressed from stuttering and stammering to being a total mute, at least for a few seconds. "Yes, I... I could do that," I responded with what I considered a Herculean effort.

I started getting dressed about 3 P.M. Actually, I started looking for something resembling clean clothes. I had some khaki pants that were hanging in the closet. I hadn't worn them since moving to Dos Cruces. I found a wadded-up white shirt in a box under the bed. Didn't smell too bad. Somewhere, I had acquired a traveling iron. It took about an hour and a half to iron the rebellious white shirt. It made several unsuccessful attempts to escape my evil clutches, but I prevailed. I put an old blue sweater vest over it, which covered most of my failings as a laundry aficionado.

I washed my old brown boots off with a dirty washcloth. Washed my old brown brush jacket off with a dirtier washcloth. I brushed my teeth, combed my hair, couldn't find cologne or aftershave. Not even Aqua Velva — and everyone knows "there's something about an Aqua Velva man." Oh well.

Looking about as spiffy as I was going to get, I headed to Laredo. The forty-five-minute drive went by in what seemed like forty-five seconds. When I got to Serrano's at 5:50 Marisol was already there. She waved me over to her table in the corner. She was having a drink — a gin and tonic it appeared. This surprised me. For some reason this surprised me a lot.

Extending her hand she rose to greet me. "Hello, Mr. Maxwell. How are you? I hope you don't mind that I started without you. I got through with my meeting a little earlier than expected."

"No, no, that's great...fine."

"Would you like something to drink?" she asked rather cheerfully. She waved the waitress over.

"Miller Lite please. Longneck if you have it," I said.

"We do," said the waitress in a not-so-cheerful voice. But at least she brought me the beer.

"Well, Mr. Maxwell. Where do we start?" Mari asked a little more seriously this time.

I hesitated and before I could get any words out, Mari continued, "Before that, can I ask you how in the world you wound up in Dos Cruces, Texas?"

"Well, my dad died a few years ago and left me six gas wells and a little house...and a lot of great memories of him. He was a neat guy. I retired from the U.S. Customs Service and didn't have much else to do or anywhere else to go. So it was Dos Cruces or Bust. That's the short version."

She was a good listener, but I'm not a good talker, so I served the conversation back into her court. "Do you mind if I ask you how in the world did you make it out of Dos Cruces?"

She laughed, spitting a few tiny drops of gin and

tonic. "Good question," she responded. "It wasn't easy."

I think Marisol Cortinas sensed that I didn't want to talk about my past, so she graciously picked up the slack in the discussion. "In a way," she said, "I was much like Angelita Cavazos. I lived with my grand-mother, but my mother was also at home with us. I knew Angelita's mother — grew up with her — and I think Angelita was probably better off without her. That probably sounds cruel, but it's true.

"My father stopped in from time to time, every cou-ple of years. He was a traveler, a gypsy. He couldn't stay in one place long. Especially if that place was Dos Cruces. He hated it there. Anyway, by the time I was in high school, my dad quit showing up at all. The last I heard he was in Washington state — around Yakima. We don't keep in touch.

"I knew I wanted out of Dos Cruces too. All kids do. It's like Alcatraz. If you don't escape by the time you're an adult, it's basically a life sentence. Anyway, I did well in school. And because of our financial situ-ation, I qualified for a full scholarship to St. Mary's. Did well there. Stayed on through law school. Anything to keep from coming back to Dos Cruces.

"I joined a large law firm in San Antonio and worked for a couple of years. My grandmother died and my mother had diabetes, so my guilt brought me back. My only concession was that I live in Catarino, not Dos Cruces. I opened up a one-woman law firm, struggled to survive, and helped look after my mother until she died — about five years ago.

"I could've moved back to San Antonio. I had

some opportunities, but I stayed on. Not sure why. Not sure I even want to know why. Then total insanity set in and I ran for District Attorney. Must be a lot of insanity in these parts, cause I somehow got elected," Marisol paused.

I was mesmerized, enchanted, bowled over, just listening to her talk. Snapping to, I asked, "What about your grandfather? Was he around when you were growing up?"

The furtively sensuous smile on her face disappeared suddenly. "Yes," she curtly replied. I did not pursue that line of questioning.

Instead, I asked, "How about a husband, fiancé, boyfriend, significant other?"

The sexy smile returned. "Not even an insignificant other. Never had the time. No, that's wrong. I had a serious beau once, in college. We even talked about getting married. But I came to the conclusion that he wasn't really ready. Of course, you probably can figure out that it was me who couldn't make the commitment. We're still friends, though. He has a wife and three beautiful children.

"And you, Mr. Maxwell, what about your family?" she asked with such sincerity. Fortunately, our grumpy waitress interrupted us and we wound up ordering supper. Saved by the dinner bell, I guess.

During supper, the conversation turned to Angelita's murder, but neither one of us had a new theory — at least, that we wanted to share. Could it be we both had been looking for pretexts to share each other's company? I certainly hoped so.

After supper, I walked her to her car in the mall

parking lot. I said something amazingly clever like, "Maybe we can do this again soon?"

She looked at me with dark, liquid eyes and a smile that would melt polar ice and quipped, "Maybe." She gave me a peck on the cheek, got in her car, and was gone. So was I — in so many ways.

Chapter 9

The Rosetta Stone

When I finally figured out that God wasn't going to leave me alone about the angel Violet, I got up, put on jeans, a long-sleeved shirt, and my beat-up hunting jacket (although I don't hunt). It was still early — 8:00 A.M. or so — and cool outside. The Dos Cruces sky was dismally gray. God and I strolled down to Dochler's place to look in on *las hermanas*.

Upon arriving at the front gate *sin* fence, I took a good look at the little house. The outside walls were adobe, and the gaps between the clay bricks, in many places, had coalesced from years of sun, wind, and rain. The structure looked as though it had spontaneously sprung from the earth, being the same color and texture. Even the wood frames around the windows and front door had a layer of burnt sienna Dos Cruces dirt to match. The only part of the house that didn't look born of nature was the rusty tin roof — and half of it was gone. Therefore, the actual living quarters were probably less than 400 square feet. I quickly calculated — for no good reason — that this amounted to 133.3333 square feet per inhabitant. Pretty cozy.

Opening the front gate, I felt a little silly, since it would have been easier to walk around it. But at least it was an icebreaker, because the ugly sister, who had been invisible behind the rusty screen door, began to scream. "Shut the goddamn gate you son-of-a-bitch! The goddamn dog'll get out! Goddamn it, can't you read the goddamn sign! Son-of-a-bitch!"

I quickly scanned the fenceless yard. No dog. I was not surprised. But I did shut the goddamn gate. And for just a second there, I did feel like a son-of-a-bitch.

Then I said, "I'm sorry ma'am, I don't have my reading glasses on so I can't read the sign. What does it say?"

"It says 'shut the gate' goddamn it. What else would it say, you son-of-a-bitch?"

"You have a point there ma'am. Did you make the sign?" I asked politely.

"No, you son-of-a-bitch. Goddamn it, you know I can't write," she snapped back.

"I forgot. I'm sorry," I said, trying my best to go along with the story that we knew each other. "I think I remember you telling me that Violet made the sign. Isn't that right?" I asked.

"You're goddamn right it is, you son-of-a-bitch," she said impatiently.

"Well, can I talk to Violet for a minute?" I implored in my sweetest fake voice.

"Goddamn it, you know she can't talk. Son-of-a-bitch. What's wrong with you? Anyway she's not here today. She went on the goddamn bus. Come back tomorrow, you son-of-a-bitch."

I knew Violet was there, but discretion being the better part of valor, especially since I had obviously committed a terminal faux pas somewhere in the ugly sister's past, I just said, "I will. Thanks."

But I now had my Rosetta Stone, hopefully, which I could use to translate the cryptic notes I'd been receiving. "SAEK TAU GOKU" spelled "shut the gate" in Violet's dialect. I would have to do some extrapolation, but it was definitely a start. The angel Violet was trying to tell me something.

Love. Let's talk about it. Like a dung beetle in the United States Congress, I'm not sure where to start. What the hell, let's start with romantic love. Please hear me through on this — especially you women. When do you think the word love was first used? Was it by a Neanderthal? Cro-magnon? A Philistine, Hittite, Egyptian? I don't know the answer, but I do know this: the word love was not first used by a man. Would any of you argue this point? Romantic love is not a concept readily understood by men. It takes a while. Usually 70 or 80 years, or past breeding age, whichever comes first.

We play the game, act the part, because we are trained by women at an early age. If you want to have sex with a woman, you must learn to use the word love. Therefore, ladies, anytime a man says the word "love," as in romantic love, you can readily substitute "want to have sex with" (i.e., I love you = I want to have sex with you). Now you can insert disclaimers and stipulations as you wish. I'm talking in generalities; there are, of course, a few exceptions.

It's not really man's fault. You can blame God. God, the Little Joker. The same God that made the act of sex equal having babies. These two events should not correlate in any way. Among other things, copulation causes overpopulation. In essence, men and women are two different species that just happen to be able to cross-pollinate. Maybe God wanted to assure His soap opera on Planet Earth would get real interesting. If love equals sex and sex equals having babies, humanity will forever writhe in turmoil. Start with two people, Adam and Eve, you got turmoil. Add a couple of kids, Cain and Abel, you got turmoil. Add a few families, then Noah and Moses, you got turmoil. Add a civilization, like the Egyptians or the Sumerians, you got turmoil. Add six billion people to a planet that can sustain five billion, you got turmoil. All because love equals sex and sex equals babies. Tell me that's not one of God's little cruelty jokes. You can rest assured that woman invented the notion of love. An abstraction beyond man's grasp. Woman, being on a much higher plane than man — which isn't saying much since man, for the most part, dwells in the nether regions — understands love. She is love.

It started with maternal instinct. Then it progressed to maternal love. And then woman thought why can't woman get that big hairy son-of-a-bitch to feel that way. Woman then had a revelation. Man likes sex. Woman will call it lovemaking, and with this simple translation, woman will train man to love.

Well, that was a couple of million years ago.

Obviously man is a pretty slow learner. Yes, God the Comedian gave men testosterone which makes him eternally horny. Then he gave women all the love hormones: estrogen, progesterone, etcetera. Then He put them together. Why would God do that? Because He didn't want to be bored. I am the exception. I learned to love Connie Lee Fitzpatrick Maxwell. Indeed, I didn't have to learn, it was instinctive and natural from Day One. She was so special, so beautiful. Of course the lust was there. It was overwhelming. But had I been a eunuch, I would have loved her. I loved her with a woman's love, real love, but I didn't know it. Or maybe I forgot. And maybe the forgetting, not the act of adultery, is the real sin for which I am being punished on this earth.

Back at St. Charles Place, I had begun the transliteration process. I felt like an Egyptologist. For those of you who have never heard of the Rosetta Stone, here's the scoop:

For many years archaeologists had been trying to interpret the hieroglyphics inscribed on Egyptian tombs and monuments. But they had nothing to go by, no starting point. In the late eighteenth century, soldiers from Napoleon's army came across a black stone near the settlement of Rosetta in Egypt.

The writing on the stone was in three languages: hieroglyphics; demotics, which was a more recent Egyptian script; and Greek. Archaeologists made the assumption, which turned out to be correct, that the three versions of the inscriptions said the same thing. Since Greek was a known language, a baseline, they were able to interpret the demotics and the hieroglyphics. My mind is filled to the brim with such minutiae. I also know that The Ohio Express recorded the song "Yummy, Yummy, Yummy, I've Got Love in My Tummy" at some point in the late 1960s.

The first thing I noticed is that the first letters in each word were the same in English and Violetian. "SAEK TAU GOKU" and "shut the gate." S. T. G. Well, I thought, that's a start.

Chapter 10

The Angel Violet, Revisited

Of course I had wondered about the weapon that killed Angelita, but since I knew Daniel was not the murderer, I figured it would never be found. I figured the real killer or killers had disposed of it in a galaxy far, far away. I figured wrong. A lot of my figuring had been pretty much totally fucked in the past few years.

So on the morning of Saturday, February 21, at exactly 2:11 A.M., I was awakened, rudely, by a combination of door pounding, screaming, flashing red lights, and the general feeling that *mi casa pequeña* was crashing down around me. The feeling was on the right track, but a shade on the side of underestimation. Actually, *mi mundo pequeño* was crashing down around me. Sheriff Arlen T. Buckner and the boys had come to pay a visit at St. Charles Place. And it wasn't of the social variety if you get my drift.

Half asleep, but rapidly gaining consciousness, I

pulled on my jeans and stumbled to the front door. I was greeted by Sheriff Buckner and ten or twelve of his good friends. And that's only the ones I could see.

"To what do I owe this pleasure?" I muttered with just a tad of sarcasm.

"Jamey Arthur Maxwell, you are under arrest for the murder of Angelita Cavazos," the good Sheriff declared in a firm and impressive voice. I detected an undertone of unadulterated glee approaching absolute rapture. This shit just keeps getting better and better for the incumbent, soon to be re-elected, High Sheriff of Losoya County.

I was not surprised by the explosion of camera flashes, nor by the glaring lights of the TV photogs, nor by the microphones being shoved in my face. TV stations from Laredo and San Antonio were there — a good story, I suppose. Buckner was playing this to the hilt. His wet dream come true. But I was surprised, and disappointed, by this: standing behind Arlen T. Buckner, Sheriff of Losoya County, was Marisol Cortinas, District Attorney of the 185th District of Texas. You see, she was up for re-election too.

Looking directly into the beautiful, but somber, brown eyes of Marisol Cortinas, I smiled a dreary smile. She didn't smile back and after a couple of seconds of eye contact, she looked down at the red-brown dirt.

The little circus sideshow lasted only a couple of minutes, but it seemed longer. Sheriff Buckner informed me that he had a search warrant for St. Charles Place. He left several of his men behind to execute said warrant. Probably wouldn't take them long to look around the petite palace.

Then I found myself, hands cuffed behind my back, in the back of Sheriff Buckner's cruiser. Chief Deputy Gilbert Ramírez was the chauffeur and Buckner was turned sideways in the shotgun seat, looking at me over his shoulder, reciting the Miranda Warning. "You have the right to remain silent…blah, blah, blah." I knew the drill — had heard myself repeat it many times over the years. But this was the first time I was on the receiving end and it's an experience I could have done without.

Arlen Buckner is not an evil man, not even a bad man, but he is a man that has been in charge of a county for so long that he believes in the doctrine of divine right. He thinks God is on his side. At this point, I was inclined to agree with him. I would have been hard pressed to come up with evidence to the contrary. My first question to Sheriff Buckner was this, "What's this all about, Arlen?" Instinctively I knew calling him by his first name was sure to piss him off, which seemed to be a continuing urge I had.

"Well, Mr. Maxwell, it seems that some of the fingerprints on the murder weapon belong to you."

As we have discussed before, one of my theories regarding the universe is that I am the only real tenant — everyone else is just a prop, robots. But now it seemed to me that I was playing the extra in someone else's universe. Maybe I'm a robot in Sheriff Arlen Buckner's cosmos. Obviously, I was not feeling well or even real. But in the event I was playing a bit part in an off–Milky Way play, I figured I might as well say my lines.

"What murder weapon?" I inquired. Pretty shitty line, I thought, but I was neither the writer nor the director. Buckner's eyebrows arched and a lopsided grin appeared. I expected him to say something like "you've got to be kidding." But he had the lead part and the best lines.

He said this instead: "Your aluminum baseball bat."

"Oh shit!" was my next line, but I chose to say it inside my spinning head.

Here's the deal: my dad loved to play baseball (mostly T-ball) with his grandkids and had purchased a bat, a hard rubber ball, and a stand about a year before his death. One day, Daniel and I had goofed around with the bat and a whiffle ball that had been left on my doorstep. A Welcome Wagon totem. The last time I had noticed the bat, it was leaning against the wooden storage shed. The only line that came to my increasingly foggy mind was, "How do you know it's my bat?" Act I of the Greek tragedy entitled The Arrest of Jamey A. Maxwell by Sheriff Arlen T. Buckner ended with this line by the good sheriff, who could hardly wait to deliver it: "Daniel Galván told me it was yours."

Suddenly, my rights under Miranda, especially the right to keep my big fucking mouth shut, seemed very important. I clammed up tighter than Dick's hatband, whatever that means. Apparently I had forgotten to give Sheriff Buckner his Miranda warning, because he was still talking.

"You know, Mr. Maxwell, your conversation with Mari... District Attorney Cortinas was very enlightening. I actually felt a little slow for not snapping on your theory earlier. Someone that knew both Daniel and Angelita, their relationship to each other, their limitations, their weaknesses. I did a little checking and found out you were once a federal agent, so I asked the Feebies to do a fingerprint check. Guess what? An exact match for four of the prints on the aluminum bat. And you know what, I was not all that surprised."

> *News bulletin-bulletin-bulletin...from station WGOD...Sheriff Arlen T. Buckner has known Marisol Cortinas in the biblical sense...they be begetting...the conjugal bed be bouncing...and so on and so forth.*

He kept talking, but I quit listening. Well, I thought, at least Daniel won't be alone for a while. That's about all I remember of the trip to Catarino. Safely in my cell after the processing — including the ever-popular strip search — I realized they were not going to let me get anywhere near Daniel. We might start concocting tall tales. Passing by his cell, I had a hasty opportunity to say, *"Hola, Daniel. Qué tal? Cómo estás, amigo?"*

Another interesting thing about Daniel: he never seems surprised. In his world anything is possible at any time, I suppose. But Daniel did look happy to see me.

"Señor Jaime! Señor Jaime!" he exclaimed and started spinning like a Tasmanian Devil. I smiled. You gotta love him, I thought. And I did.

It was no coincidence that I was arrested early in the weekend when no judge or magistrate would be available for arraignment. Not until Monday, at the earliest. As a Customs Agent, I had pulled this stunt many times myself. Generally, you use this tactic on people you really don't like and/or believe deserve just a little extra punishment. Could it be Sheriff Buckner felt this way about *moi*? Maybe.

I used my first phone call to contact an attorney, but not the one you would expect. The attorney I called first was District Attorney Marisol Cortinas. My second call was to my obscene, but extremely competent attorney, Jimmy Boyer. Of course, I got to speak to two answering machines in a row. My message to both of them was brief: "I'm in the Catarino stockade. We need to talk ASAP."

Fortunately, Jimmy B. was already scheduled to visit Daniel on Monday, March 2, so he could kill two jailbirds with one stone. At this point, I was more interested in a dialogue with Marisol Cortinas. I had a bone or two — of the Brachiosaurus variety — to pick with her. Anger, disappointment, and puzzlement were the top three sensations, but I couldn't tell which would win, place, or show. To my amazement, she showed up at 8:00 A.M. Monday morning.

Marisol was lead into the interrogation room by a nondescript jail guard. I had already been ushered to my reserved seat behind the gray metal Formica-topped table. Wearing jailbird orange and cuffs, I was literally all dressed up with no place to go. She pulled up a seat on the other side and before I could say a word, she turned and instructed the guard to leave us alone. Surprisingly he did so.

Marisol looked so serious, I almost laughed, but I wasn't really in that sort of mood. After an uncomfortable pause, I started, "I just have two questions: Why? And how long have you been fucking Arlen Buckner?" I was obviously even madder than I thought. She was caught off guard, probably by the second question. "My personal life is none of your business. Who do you think you are? You don't even know me." Well, so much for the small talk, I thought.

"And as far as your being arrested, I hardly think you can blame me or Sheriff Buckner, for that matter, for doing our jobs. And if you do, tough shit." I had the urge to say "you sure are cute when you cuss," but I stifled it. I figured this to be a short conversation, but again, I figured wrong. "You're right, your personal life is not my business. I apologize. But I notice you have not denied the allegations. Sorry. Strike that last comment from the record." I was becoming a Babylonian, as Big Al would say. Getting arrested for first-degree murder probably has that effect on a lot of people.

Marisol cracked a tiny, short-lived smile and said, "Mr. Maxwell, I went to Sheriff Buckner because you had convinced me that we should at least consider the possibility that another person had killed Angelita and then framed Daniel. It was plausible and you were very convincing. You were never a suspect in my mind, but let me assure you: if you did murder Angelita Cavazos, I will put you away. Maybe have you executed. It's my job and I intend to do it."

Toward the end of this short monologue, Mari

sounded like a little girl. Ms. Cortinas sounded as if she were trying to persuade herself as much as me. I knew then that Marisol, the person, the woman, did not believe Jamey Maxwell, the prime suspect, was guilty. Feeling better. Feeling good.

"Now I'm going to tell you some things that I shouldn't. Things that could cause me to lose my job — to be permanently disbarred from practicing law. I should not even be here talking to you at this moment. Especially without witnesses. And I'm not sure why I'm doing this. I've worked very hard and have overcome a lot of obstacles to get where I am.

"Do you know how hard it was for a woman, particularly a Hispanic woman, to get elected District Attorney in this part of the world? Even things like my size and my height were questioned. It wasn't just a matter of politics. It was a matter of paying my dues. It was a matter of public perception. It was a matter of swallowing my pride and biting my tongue when I really didn't want to. I had to play the game, but it's been worth it, because I know I'm doing a good job. I know I'm making a difference. No one has to tell me that."

This speech sounded rehearsed and I knew why. She had been over this in her head many times, so to that extent, it was rehearsed. Mari was looking at me as she spoke, but I wasn't sure she saw me. If she did, Ms. Cortinas would have seen me smiling at her.

She continued, "When I was elected four years ago, people thought it was a fluke. Especially my opponent and his supporters. They claimed election fraud, payoffs, dead people voting, all of the things that once were a part of politics in Losoya County and the 185th District.

"But the truth is, I beat him at his own game. My platform was tougher enforcement of existing laws, mandatory sentencing, fewer parolees, and putting violent offenders behind bars. Lauro Soliz thought he had the election won. His machismo wouldn't let him think otherwise. A stereotypical, Mexican male — always looking down on women. Thinking their only function should be in the kitchen and the bedroom and he gets to decide which and at what time! *Pendejo! Pinche bato!*"

My presence was no longer necessary for this conversation to continue. Marisol was on a roll! But I wouldn't have missed it for the world.

"That son-of-a-bitch thought the job was his. That he didn't even have to campaign. Just go hunting and drinking with his *cuñyados*. The bastard even had the nerve to ask me out during the campaign. Said he may even have a job for me after the election. '*Chinga tu madre*, you arrogant fuck!' That's what I told him and he laughed in my face. But I kicked his macho ass in the election and I've been kicking it in court since then. Fuck him! Fuck all of them!"

Mari regained consciousness and actually saw me. By that time I was grinning from ear to ear, so she said, "And fuck you too!"

I started laughing, hard, and she joined in. What a bizarre little scene. I wondered what the guard right outside the door was thinking. But then again, I really didn't give a shit. After the laughter died down, Mari grew serious. She told me, "Mister, here's the deal.

Besides the baseball bat with your fingerprints, Sheriff Buckner has established that you were one of the last people, if not the last, to see Angelita Cavazos alive. She left Reynaldo's at approximately 10:00 P.M. She was going to walk home. I understand that was not unusual. Her grandmother says you were the last customer to leave that night, about thirty minutes earlier. The Millers have both given statement that at 2:17 A.M. they saw what they believe was an Anglo male, fitting your description, carrying something in Daniel's goat pen. At the time, they thought it was a goat. They did not come forward voluntarily because they didn't want to get involved."

I stopped Mari and asked, "Who in the hell are the Millers?"

"They're the people that live next door to Daniel's place. In the pretty little white frame house. The one with the picket fence."

I laughed, "The Millers huh? What a great all-American name. I wonder where they got it? I wonder if the real Millers are still alive?"

Marisol gave me a perplexed glance and continued, "Anyway, that, along with some statements that Daniel has supposedly given, makes you one hell of a suspect."

"How are they getting this information from Daniel? You know how he is. What are they doing? Who's asking the questions?"

"Mostly Gilbert Ramírez, Arlen's Chief Deputy. Daniel seems to like him. They use Spanish, Tex-Mex, hand gestures, charades, whatever."

"Will that stand up in court?" I asked.

"Probably not" she responded, "but you never know. I will have to try to introduce it."

I looked at her closely and said, "You shouldn't be telling me this."

"Duhhh. What do think I was talking about earlier, Mister?"

Well, it was confirmed. Mister was my new pet name from Marisol Cortinas. Cool. It sounded sexy when she said it. I looked into her eyes and softly said, "I've got a question, but I'm not sure how to ask it."

Mari said, "Just ask it dammit. And make it fast. I've been here too long already."

So I asked, "How exactly did Daniel confess to the rape and murder of Angelita? I don't think he even knows what either one is really."

"He didn't use words," Mari replied, "he used gestures."

"What were they?" I asked and began to get a very uneasy feeling.

Marisol then demonstrated the universal sign for fucking, and the universal sign for killing, and I wanted to wriggle out of my totally goose-bumped skin. But, instinctively, I kept my mouth shut.

Mari said, "Before I go, Mister, I want to share this, quickly. Arlen Buckner is not the person you think he is. He's a good man who has been through some bad times. His twelve-year-old daughter died of leukemia five years ago. It almost killed him. The strain of the guilt and grief was too much for his marriage.

"His wife left him three years later. But the marriage was over the day his daughter died. He was up for re-election the same year I ran for District

Attorney. He was one of the few people with political influence in Losoya County who supported me. He suffered for it, but I don't think he cared at the time. He didn't even care if he lived or died. It's probably the only reason he endorsed me. The timing was right. I was sympathetic, even empathetic with him. Not many people were, mostly because they didn't know what to say or do.

"Yes, we had a thing for a while but it didn't last long and didn't do any permanent damage. It may have even helped both of us. . . in different ways. He's a good man and a good sheriff. You've given him a reason for living again. He just happens to be totally convinced you're guilty of murdering Angelita Cavazos. And you can't really blame him, can you?"

She didn't let me answer. She finished with this: " And you, of all people, Mister, should know what it's like to be in Arlen Buckner's shoes."

With that parting bull's-eye, she turned and left Jamey Maxwell dazed, confused, and not just a little horny.

At 2:47 P.M., Gentleman Jim Boyer showed up and I was escorted back to the interrogation room. He politely asked the same nondescript guard to leave us alone. "Hey, asshole, give us a break here. My client and I want to have sex and we feel uncomfortable with you watching us." I love Jimmy Boyer. Not in that way, but I love him nevertheless.

"Well Maxwell, what the fuck?"

"Would you believe it's all a terrible mistake, Jimmy, my man?"

"More like a Bulgarian bundle fuck wouldn't you

say?" he retorted. Jimmy B. is so original. "Give me the straight skinny. Mainline me," said Jimmy B. So I did.

He interrupted frequently to get more details, to get the skinny straighter. I felt better just talking to him. I didn't bother to mention my conversation earlier in the day with D.A. Cortinas. I had made an implicit promise to be discreet and even though I trusted Jimmy Boyer with my life, literally, and I knew attorney-client privilege would be paramount, I intended to keep my tacit promise to Mari C.

Tuesday morning, my main man, the man I would most likely have sex with if I were a woman, Jimmy Boyer, had a bond reduction motion before Judge Arturo Durán. By that afternoon, I was in court in my fluorescent orange prison togs standing before His Honor, Judge Durán, with Gentleman Jim Boyer by my side. This was James Boyer's universe. His luminescence bounced off the dark, grimy walls of the Losoya County courtroom. The courtroom was his battlefield of dreams and the place he had been knighted Gentleman Jim.

Across the worn gray linoleum tiles from us stood District Attorney Marisol Cortinas and Sheriff Arlen Buckner. I tried not to look their way because I was afraid I would smile at both of them — for entirely different reasons. But I did risk a sidelong glance and saw Mari looking down at her notes. I thought she was glancing sideways at me, but I couldn't be sure. She looked like a little girl playing dress up in her gray pinstriped power suit. I smiled, but only on the inside.

Daniel was not there because Jimmy Boyer did not want to allow shadows to fall across Judge Arturo Durán's shiny, bald head. He did not want to confuse His Honor and give him any reason to deny bail. Even though we knew Daniel was not a "flight risk," Jimmy figured, and rightly so, that the judge might consider him just that. This is another form of discrimination which should have been wiped out long ago, but hasn't been and may not ever be. Because Daniel is Hispanic and lives close to the Mexican border, he is considered a risk. No matter that he and his entire family are mentally retarded and would be just as likely to build a spaceship and fly to Uranus than find their way to Mexico. And this from a Hispanic judge to boot.

Jimmy Boyer intended to fight Daniel's battle later in the week. "I like to slip it in a little at a time," he said with a salacious leer. Jimmy Boyer is consistent as a lawyer, as a friend, and as a pervert. If Daniel and I were considered at the same time, it might be easy for Judge Durán to say no to both of us. A package deal, or rather a package no deal. Gentleman Jim's instincts were tracking well, but not without a lot of help and one helluva shock from D.A. Cortinas.

Here's what transpired that day in the shabby Losoya County courtroom: after the customary "Oye, Oye bullshit," Jimmy Boyer presented this motion to Judge Durán.

"Your Honor, my client, Mr. Jamey Maxwell, comes before you today with a respectful and just request. Mr. Maxwell served an enduring and distinguished career, with numerous accolades, as a Special

Agent/Criminal Investigator with the United States Department of the Treasury. More than 25 years, Your Honor, without the slightest blemish.

"I personally had the privilege of working with him toward the honorable goal of protecting our country from those who would do it harm. I, as the former United States Attorney for the Western District of Texas, would literally lay my life on the line for this man.

"Your Honor, my client is totally guiltless, not only of the crime for which he has been charged, but of any and all crimes, including parking tickets." At this point, I couldn't resist turning and looking at Mari. She was trying her best to stifle an adorable little grin. Sheriff Buckner, on the other hand, was turning an interesting shade of mauve.

"Special Agent in Charge Maxwell, now retired, had, until this unfortunate misunderstanding, an immaculate official record of personal behavior. I feel confident that the Honorable Sheriff Buckner can attest to that fact after conducting due diligence research.

"Therefore, my client requests that his bond be set at $500,000, which he considers fair to all parties involved. And, Your Honor, I would be honored to co-sign the bond with Mr. Maxwell, to show how much confidence and faith I have in my client. Thank you, Your Honor." Jimmy hadn't mentioned he was going to do that — made me feel good.

Judge Durán spoke, "Miss Cortinas, what do you have to say about the request from Mr. Boyer on behalf of his client, Jamey Maxwell?"

There was a pause — maybe 15 seconds, seemed longer though. Then District Attorney Marisol Cortinas, who had been looking down at the old faux mahogany table in front of her, looked up at Judge Arturo Durán and said these words: "I have no objection Your Honor. I consider it to be a fair request."

I'm not sure who was most shocked by this statement: Jimmy Boyer, Judge Durán, Sheriff Buckner, or me. I think it probably fell pretty much in that order. But there is no doubt who was most pissed off. It was my good friend Arlen. His complexion had progressed from mauve to an interesting shade of purple. Oh well.

It took several hours to get the bond arranged, so I waited, not so patiently, back in my cell. It was nice when freedom came. I had given Jimmy Boyer my power of attorney and a personal check for $50,000 (10% of the bond). He had money wired from his account in Houston, converted to a cashier's check, and bonded me out. Free at last, free at last, thank God almighty. . .

The bad news was Jimmy was unable to secure bond for Daniel — at any amount. Judge Durán ordered Daniel held without bond because D.A. Cortinas (probably in an attempt to soothe Arlen Buckner's savage brow) protested on the basis that Daniel would be a flight risk. No surprise, just disappointment. Mari also felt, I'm quite sure, that Daniel would be safer behind bars at this point, since there had been threats made in Dos Cruces. The source of the threats was unclear — probably just some of the local *batos* talking in their *cerveza*. But Ms. Cortinas was probably right, even though I had planned for Daniel to stay with me if he got out. My track record of protecting the people close to me was far from commendable.

It was six o'clock and growing dark when I finally returned to St. Charles Place. And guess what? I had another little package — an old cracked teapot — waiting on my little porch. I knew who it was from and was now extremely interested to see what message awaited. But first, I needed my thinking juice. I popped the ring on a sensuously cold Miller Lite, took a swig, and then lifted the lid on the little white China teapot with pink roses.

The electromagnetic signals being sent by the Big Guy through the Angel Violet were getting stronger. I sensed, down to my weary bones, that this new communiqué was significant. And that it was connected to the murder of Angelita Cavazos. On a neatly folded piece of paper torn from a Big Chief tablet (just like the one I had) were these hieroglyphics: "DOMXYHS 6, BECXAILDUR 5." It was time for the Rosetta Stone.

I got out my Big Chief tablet. One of the pages had been torn and surprise, surprise, it matched the note from Violet. But strangely, instead of feeling like my privacy had been Violated, so to speak, I felt calm and reassured. I then got out the three other notes that had been left on my doorsteps. I then deduced the following:

Since "SAEK TAU GOKU" = "shut the gate," and the first letter of each word appeared to be correct, then: $S = s$; $A = h$; $E = u$; $K = t$; T also $= t$ if used as first letter of a word; $A = h$ again; $U = e$; $G = g$; $O = a$; $K = t$

again; *U* = *e* again.

Dear God and Violet, couldn't you make this a little easier?

Anyway, based on this, the first note, "I SOM TAUW" = "I sa_ the_."

The second note, "TARUU OB TAUW" = "th_ee o_ the_."

"LOS DIABLOS," the third note, appeared to mean just that, "The Devils."

The note I had just received, "DOMXYHS 6, BECX-AILDUR 5" = "da_ _ _ _ _ 6, bu_ _h_ _ _ e_ 5"

I decided to try this: in the blanks, where I wasn't sure of the conversion, I would use the letters Violet used. Here's what it looked like:

Note 1: "I sam thew"

Note 2: "three ob thew"

Note 3: "Los Diablos"

Note 4: "damxyhs 6, bucxhilder 5"

Immediately, I went to Note 2. "Ob" had to be "of." So now I have "three of thew." I took a wild-ass guess and changed *w* to *m*. "Three of them."

I then went to Note 1. "I sam them," I changed to "I saw them."

So far it made sense. "I saw them." "Three of them." "Los Diablos."

Now for Note 4. It seemed *M* = *w*. So "damxyhs" becomes "dawxyhs." Now I have "dawxyhs 6, bucx-hilder 5." Dawxyhs 6 and Bucxhilder 5 sounded like an intergalactic baseball score, but it wasn't.

I already knew what "bucxhilder 5" meant. It was one of the wells I had inherited from my dad, the Buckholder #5. And since I had visited that well, recently, with my dad's old friend and contract gauger, Howard Overstreet, I was able to solve the rest of the riddle. "Dawxyhs 6" was Dawkins #6 drilling rig, which just so happened to have completed a dry hole within the last week. It was a well drilled to offset the Buckholder #5 by another investor-owned/investor-screwed (investors *pobrecitos*) oil company. The rig was still on-site, less than a quarter of a mile from my Buckholder #5.

I took a quick shower to wash off the aroma of Essence de Catarino Stockade; passed a quick toothbrush through my funky-tasting mouth; slipped on some old jeans, sweatshirt, brush jacket, and boots; hopped in the S-10 truckita and headed two miles north of town to the Buckholder lease.

I had made several trips to this and my other five wells with Howard Overstreet. He had even shown me a few things about the wells so I could check them myself if he was unavailable. I already knew a little bit about gauging from riding around with my dad from time to time. I knew how to open a valve to relieve pressure, how to gauge a tank, and how to change a chart on the gas meter.

It was dark when I drove past the Buckholder #5, through an open gate to the Dawkins #6 drilling rig. I was still on the Buckholder lease, which comprised about 5,000 acres. A late model Ford F350 diesel truck with all the amenities — brush guard, tool box, deer rifle, bumper sticker that read "drillers do it deeper," etcetera — was parked in front of what is commonly called a doghouse. A doghouse, in oilfield terms, is a small, portable building used for an office by various, sundry oilfield folks — especially on drilling rigs. This one was made out of corrugated tin. It's usually the last thing removed from a drilling site aside from the rig itself. There was a light on inside.

I knocked on the door and was rewarded with a gruff "come in." Opening the door, I was instantly greeted by the odor combo of Jack Daniels Whisky, Marlboro cigarettes, diesel oil, old clothes, and other smells best left unidentified.

"What can I do you for," asked the crusty old gentleman behind the crusty old gray desk — both coated with layers of grease, grime, smoke, and cynicism. He looked to be somewhere between fifty and one hundred and fifty years old. The old fart didn't even bother to look up. He was "the driller" on the Dawkins #6 rig. How did I know he was the driller? Three reasons: he looked like one (they all look alike); he smelled like one (as mentioned); and God told me so.

"My name's Maxwell," I said extending my hand.

The building was no more than six and a half feet high and eight feet wide, so when I walked through the door, I was standing right in front of him. He still didn't bother to look up, even though I'm sure he saw not only my outstretched hand, but my entire persona. He just kept on writing what I'm sure were reports that should have been completed weeks ago.

These guys — these drillers — live hard lives of hard drinking, hard smoking, hard fighting, and hard fucking. So they tend to get a little hardheaded, not to mention rude. So believe me when I say, like old whores, they don't give a fuck for nothing. Knowing small talk would do nothing but make this crusty old bastard crustier, I got right to the point.

"What can you tell me about Los Diablos?" I asked.

His writing hand slowed to a rolling stop and he finally looked up at me.

"You a cop?" he growled.

"Can't even spell it," I calmly responded.

He grinned a gapped-tooth grin that exposed yellow stains on the teeth that remained and brown tobacco juice dripping at the corners. "Fired their sorry asses two days ago. Woulda done it sooner, but can't get no help, 'cept for Meskins in these parts. Fired 'um soon as we td'd." That meant total depth — when they got to the bottom of the hole.

"Had to pull string short-handed, but better than paying those worthless fuckers for standing around with their thumbs up their hungover asses," he pleasantly explained. "Axelrod was a pretty decent pusher when he was sober. But that was about as rare as virgin pussy around this shit-hole country. Now, Doobie and the fat Meskin weren't worth a fuck no time, drunk or sober."

We've all heard the expression "it made my skin crawl," but this was the first time I had actually felt it. I fully expected to see exposed bloody muscle tissue when I looked down at my arm and my skin outside, lying underneath a mesquite tree. The name Axelrod by itself didn't ring my chimes, but when coupled with Doobie, my brain ignited.

The old codger was still babbling about the shitty world and all the shitty people that inhabit it, but God was using the inside of my skull as a movie screen. He was replaying a cold night at Reynaldo's two years ago. Jesus, Mary, and Joseph, this could not be real. But it was. It was. I think it was.

"Do you know where I could find them?" I solemnly asked.

"Find who?" was the old coot's response.

He had gone way past Los Diablos and was all the way down to his son-in-law on the list of worthless fucks in the world.

"Axelrod and his friends," I replied.

"Sure. At Zenia's Place in Catarino gettin' drunk with some old Meskin whores," he hissed.

"By the way, why are they called Los Diablos?" I asked, already knowing the real answer.

"The stupid fuckers all got drunk one night and had it tattoed on their arms. Showed up here still drunk and showed all the other fuckers, like they was special shitasses or somthin'." For a second there I thought I had been mistaken about Violet bestowing the name of Los Diablos upon these miserable three. Then it came to me in a whisper: she had not only named them, she had them brand themselves with the mark of the devil. It seems the angel Violet possessed more powers than I had realized. I thanked the loquacious driller and I was gone.

My mind was attempting to accept the ramifications of what I had just heard, but my thoughts kept fragmenting. The emotional shrapnel hurt — made it hard to focus. Visions of dead and dying angels with faces I could not bear to recognize.

God said, "Go see Violet."

Okay. Yes.

It wasn't until I was standing inside my little living room that I regained a modicum of awareness. The light in the kitchen was on. I was holding Violet's notes and saying something about Angelita. I asked God to forgive me for what I was about to do. I think He said, "I will, My Son, I will."

Time had passed, maybe an hour. I had changed clothes. I wasn't sure why. But I knew where I was going. Down three Dos Cruces blocks to Violet's house. Total darkness enveloped me as I walked to Old Dochler's place. It was a cool night, but someone had dressed me in my nicest (and only) wool sports coat. The coolness and the blackness felt comforting and I experienced a vague and pleasant flashback to a night when I was yet a child. Sometime before my ninth birthday, when the world was still blameless. Now, I was standing in front of an angel's adobe abode.

"Violet, I need to talk to you. Please." No answer. The earthy house was totally dark. It must have been close to midnight, but that didn't matter at this point.

"Los Diablos, Violet," louder this time.

A flicker of light through the small window beside the door. A match lighting a candle. Then the bellowing started.

"Goddamn, son-of-a-bitch, we're trying to sleep in here! What do you want this time you son-of-a-bitch? How many times do I have to tell you we're not going back with you, goddamn it!"

"Please, I just need to talk to Violet for a second. I know you're not going back with me, I understand," I said, playing my part in her soap opera, "But I've got to talk to Violet."

"She ain't here you goddamn son-of-a-bitch," the old biddy wailed.

But she was, she was standing right behind the crazy one, her alabaster face and gray-white mane glimmering in the candlelight, a halo effect — or was it a halo? She was looking at the universe above my head.

Violet's sister was still babbling non-stop. Something about how I never should have left them and I'm relatively certain she was still impugning my mammalian lineage while simultaneously using the Lord's name in vain. But by this point, I was focused totally on Violet, wondering how I could get through to her. Then I decided to let God do His fair share. So for several minutes I just stood under the cool, dark Dos Cruces sky exhaling my foggy thoughts, letting them float up to the ether, the upper atmosphere, where Violet's thoughts resided. Of course the crazy old loon was still standing in front of Violet denying that she was there. And for the most part, that was true. Yes, it was.

"God sent me, Violet. You already know that," is how I began. "Just like He sent you to help me find the men who killed Angelita. I got your notes, Violet, and it took me a while, but I finally figured them out. I know their names. Los Diablos... I know who they are, Violet. Luther Axelrod and the two others. And I know they're evil and I know they must be punished for their sins. I know what the punishment is and I know I am the one who must carry it out. I'm speaking the truth, aren't I Violet? This is what He requires

— this is what I must do."

And even though the old crone was still scolding me, I was enveloped in a protective cloak of perfect silence. The Dos Cruces night became deathly tranquil. Then Violet's gaze slowly, dreamily, lowered and her eyes met mine. Time ceased to exist. The world as I had known it became irrelevant. There was only Violet and me... and God. The answer came in the manifestation of the most radiant yet profoundly sad smile an earthling had ever seen. Violet turned away from the shimmering candle and disappeared.

The sun was shining though the kitchen window at St. Charles Place when I regained consciousness. I had obviously made it back home from Violet's shack. Apparently, I had been sitting in my tiny kitchen at my tiny table for hours in total darkness. And total oblivion. Maybe my soul had gone to speak with God. If so, it must have been on neutral territory, because neither my eyes nor the eyes of my soul would ever see the gates of Heaven. This much I knew.

But preternatural momentum had taken hold of Jamey Maxwell and required that I keep moving — I would say forward, but it felt more like downward — toward the abyss. Voices, now more than one, were telling me to go to... Marisol. I really did not want to drag her into this any... any deeper than she already.... Focus, I had to stay focused, but it was growing increasingly difficult.

I lied to you earlier... about Marisol Cortinas and me being drawn to each other for no apparent reason. There was a damn good reason, I just didn't want to talk about it. We have a secret in common. She, too, had suffered deeply at some time during her child-hood. God told me as soon as her eyes first met mine. I could tell by her pupils. The blackness was so black, the emptiness so empty, but I chose to ignore it. I could not — or did not want to — see the relevance.

And, per God's edification, there was now someone besides Mari who shared this abysmal secret. God had reminded me of my own suffering and instead of choosing to ignore it, I completely denied it, and wish I could still. It sickened me, disgusted me, pissed me off, made me hate myself, and made me hate God for telling me.

I called Marisol at her office in Catarino. "I need to see you," I whispered. My normal voice had deserted me and I'm sure this sounded like an obscene phone call. But even though I had not identified myself, Mari knew it was me.

"What's wrong?" she asked in a way that conveyed more than a little trepidation.

"I've got to see you now," was all I could reply.

"Meet me at my house. Three-eleven Agarita. Five blocks north of the courthouse. Where are you?" she asked.

"I'll be there in twenty minutes," I said.

She answered the door still dressed for work, and to her I must have looked like the madman that I was.

"What's wrong? What's going on?" she asked almost crying. She knew that I knew something dreadful.

"I know who killed Angelita. Violet told me," I was barely able to whisper.

"Violet, the crazy sister?" Mari responded, almost

pleading. She continued, "How does she know who did it? She can't even talk. How did she tell you? Did she see them?"

"Yes, she saw them, but not in the way you think. God showed her. He... He gave her a vision."

"What are you talking about? What do you... who killed... Angelita?" Mari stuttered.

"I will not tell you that. I should not have come to see you... there's no proof... there's nothing you can do. No, that's wrong. There is something you can do, but only if something happens to me. If something happens, go to Violet. Tell her God sent you. She will tell you what you need to know. She will see what she needs to see in your eyes. And then she will tell you.

"Only do this if you are unable to contact me for more than three days. Do you understand, Mari? Promise! Unless I'm gone for more than three days," my voice was getting stronger. Mari was afraid to say anything except, "I promise." But her fear was for me, not for herself.

I returned to my father's house, St. Charles Place, which no longer seemed like mine. I now belonged nowhere, or at the very least, I belonged somewhere else. God was calling the shots and He would not let me rest until His will be done. Peace and comfort would no longer be a possibility for Jamey Maxwell — if it ever was. You see, God's deal with me was to punish me here on earth for my sins, so I wouldn't go to Hell. There was nothing in the contract about my going to Heaven. A slight oversight on my part.

Chapter 11

I, The Avenging Angel

Hate. Let's talk about it. Hate can be one hell of a motivator, but it tends to be all-consuming. With hate growing in your spiritual garden, once it has reached full bloom, all other emotions are forced into dormancy. It is one sentiment that is difficult to ignore. And if it is fed to you in ever-increasing portions — kind of like a giant shit sandwich, by a very angry God — it's downright impossible to ignore.

I conceived hate on my ninth birthday. It incubated for forty-one years, the incubus thereupon bursting forth, full-grown, to the detriment of Los Diablos. The placenta shriveled inside my soul leaving a precarious void, a hollow, a tantalizing vacuum for all manner of opportunistic emotions, from the virtuous to the perverse. To date, I am still uncertain which of God's blessings and/or curses has taken root.

To say the murders of Jacinto Ocala, Dwayne DuBois, and Luther Axelrod were premeditated would be a bit of an understatement. Actually, the murders were preordained — by God. So if I get sentenced to forty years in the electric chair, He's going with me.

An old movie with Frank Sinatra and Laurence Harvey, "The Manchurian Candidate," is about an American POW who is brainwashed by his Chinese captors to assassinate a politician upon his return to the United States. I guess you could call me the Dos Crucian Candidate with the following qualifier: I was brainwashed by the Head Brainwasher to assassinate three motherfuckers even lower than a politician.

Waiting until dark, I drove back to Catarino, this time to Zenia's Place. To keep me company, I had brought along Taz and a twelve-pack of Miller Lite. I figured it would be a long night, so I found a dark place next to a dark deserted shack, parked, and popped a ring on a cold one. The pooch looked thirsty. I gave him the first swig.

Hours passed. Around 11:00 P.M., a Diablo came walking out of Zenia's. It was Jacinto Ocala, Chango — I would recognize him anywhere. Even in Hell. He was corpulent and he was evil.

God told me something else. Jacinto Ocala had no soul. He was not human, and, having no soul, if he went to Hell he would not suffer. He would just be there — as a spectator I suppose.

It seemed that Los Diablos were Hell's equivalent of the three characters from the Wizard of Oz: the tin man, the lion, and the scarecrow. But in this case, instead of having no heart, no courage, and no brain; Chango had no soul, Doobie had no balls, and Luther had no . . . respect for me. And Satan — like the Wizard of Oz — would not be able to give them these things. "Taz, I don't think we're in Kansas anymore."

Chango was staggering down the Catarino dirt street — fortunately or unfortunately, depending on who was pondering it — by himself. I started up my truck and pulled alongside him. In the darkness, it would be impossible for him to recognize me.

"*Hola, Chango. Qué pasa, cuñyado?*" I said in my very best Tex-Mex.

"*Nada*. Who's there?" he slurred.

"*Muerte,*" I replied. Death.

"What the fuck?" Chango asked.

He had stopped in the middle of the road and was gawking, trying to see inside the truck.

"Closer, *mi amigo,*" I enticed. He took a wobbly step toward me and was now close enough.

Reaching out my window, I grabbed the thick mane of black, nasty hair and pulled his head down sharply. Blood flew as his forehead met the drip rim of the truck door. What an unpleasant sound.

Swiftly, I was out of the truck and while Chango was still stunned, I whacked him upside the head with my gun. Thank God — literally, I think — he didn't go down. But he was dazed, confused and now at my mercy. *Pobrecito!* I led him around to the back of my truck and with the tailgate down forced Chango to slide into the bed. He was horizontal and losing consciousness. I tied his feet and hands together behind his back. The hog was hogtied. I noticed that Taz had jumped into the bed of the truck with me and was intently observing the goings on. I stepped down onto the dirt street and closed the tailgate. Taz joined me and we were back inside the cab headed south.

We drove through Dos Cruces and onto the Buckholder lease. I stopped at the Buckholder #5 tank battery. Taz and I got out to check on our cargo. It was moving around, moaning and cussing. It was not happy cargo. Oh well.

The clouds had cleared in the brush country sky and overhead a half moon appeared to be mocking... I wasn't sure whom. I rolled Chango out of the truck and he hit the dirt with a thud. I cut the ropes around his hands and feet, stood back several paces and recommended that Chango get to his feet. He struggled to do so — he was still not thinking clearly. The anesthetic effect of the booze was wearing off, though, and Chango was grumpy.

"What the fuck's going on!" Chango screamed at me. "Who the fuck are you?" He took a step toward me. I cranked off a round of 9mm inches from his feet. Chango jumped several feet high. Not bad for a fat guy.

"I'm gonna kill you, motherfucker!" he was stumbling around, still screaming at me.

"I doubt that," I replied.

"Who are you... what do you fucking want from me?" he bellowed.

"Your life. But first some information," I said.

"I know you, you're Maxwell," Chango remembered. "We should've killed you when we had the chance!"

"Probably," I answered.

Jacinto Ocala was starting to calm down. And for

some reason, getting his confidence up. I guess I just didn't look that mean to him. But I was. Meaner than he could ever imagine.

"So, motherfucker, what is it?" he sneered. "What information?"

"I want you to tell me about how you and Luther and that other shithead killed Angelita Cavazos. I want the details," I replied.

"I don't know what the fuck you're talking about you crazy son-of-a-bitch. You're the one that killed her."

Wrong answer, fat boy. This time I shot a little closer. Again, Chango jumped pretty high.

"You better kill me, motherfucker, cause I'm gonna kill you first chance I get," he threatened.

"Oh, I'm gonna kill you, but first you're gonna tell me the story I need to hear," I said.

"Fuck you," was his response.

Again, wrong answer. This time I shot Chango's toad-like, chubby right foot. It went splat. This time he wanted to jump, he just couldn't. Instead, he screamed.

"You shot me! Motherfucker... you shot my foot!"

"Tell me about killing Angelita," I commanded, "or I'll shoot your balls off."

"Okay, okay," Chango said, falling to the ground. "Jesus Christ, you crazy bastard."

"Start talking... now." I pointed the gun just below his abundant midsection.

Chango looked at me. He finally realized that I just might kill him. "It was Luther's idea. We were drinking one night and talking about what you had done to us at the café in Dos Cruces. I didn't think he was crazy enough to go through with it. Just figured we would drive down to Dos Cruces and scare some people." Chango paused.

I nudged him along with my Model 59 and he continued, "Anyway, Luther told Dwayne to drive by your place to see if you were home. The lights were out so we figured you were at Reynaldo's. Luther got out and looked around your garage and came back with a baseball bat."

"Keep going."

"We drove by Reynaldo's and could see you through the window. We waited until you left and until the girl started walking home."

"When she got a couple of blocks from the café, Dwayne pulled up beside her. I grabbed her and put her in the backseat. Luther told Dwayne to drive out to the rig." Chango, still holding his bloody foot, paused to rock back and forth, moaning.

"Finish the story," I said.

"He figured you owned this well. The sign on the tank battery said 'Maxwell and Sons Oil and Gas.' He figured that had to be you. Not too many Maxwells in Dos Cruces. So he told Dwayne to stop here. That's where we did the girl."

"What did you do?" I asked, the fire inside me growing.

Chango grinned a malicious grin, his anger apparently overcoming his fear for the moment. "So you want the details you sick motherfucker? Okay, I'll give 'em to you. Luther told me to tie her to that tree over there," he pointed to a big mesquite about 50 feet away. "We had brought some rope...(Chango was still talking, but flashes of anguish exploded inside my head...a young boy tied to a tree...two guys...) pulled her pants off...(pulling his jeans off...) Luther did her first, then me, then Dwayne...(squirming, moaning, begging them to stop...) We left her there and drank some beer in the car. It was pretty fucking cold...(shaking, it's so cold, so cold...) after a while, Luther says let's do her again...Dwayne didn't want to...she was...(begging them to stop...) so I fucked her again...then Luther laughs and says he's gonna give it to her in the ass...(please, God...) the girl was screaming, begging him to stop...but Luther was just...(laughing and moaning...) the crazy mother-fucker was just laughing and moaning."

My awareness, my focus returned to Chango. "Then what," I demanded.

Maybe Chango thought by telling this story he could shock me into inaction. With a sadistic smile still planted on his fat face, he continued, "Luther told me to go get her. I cut the rope and brought her back to the car. She was conscious, but she wasn't saying anything. Wasn't even crying. Luther told me to carry her up to the top of the tank battery...(He pointed to the two 400 barrel tanks, they were about twenty feet high with a steel ladder and landing) carried her up to the top. Luther told me to hold her by the feet over the edge...him and Dwayne were laughing...so I held her like that...then Luther said drop her...thought he was kidding, but he wasn't...he yelled at me to drop her...so I did...she never made a sound 'til she hit the dirt...then just a groan and her neck cracking."

"Then Luther brought your baseball bat over and hit her in the head. But she was already dead. He did that just to frame your ass. Worked pretty fucking good, eh?" Chango was displaying a bad attitude. Was he forgetting how tenuous his situation was? Probably.

"We put her in the trunk. We drove to the crazy guy's house — with all his fucking goats — and Luther put her in the goat pen. Then we hauled ass.

"That's the whole fucking story, so are you happy now, motherfucker?"

Evidently, Chango still didn't understand how this was going to go down. He thought getting shot in the foot and having to hobble back to Dos Cruces was the worst that was going to happen to him. What a maroon!

"Get up," I yelled.

Chango was startled. "Hey man, I told you the story. Just leave me alone!" he demanded unconvincingly.

Before I could say "get up" again, Taz, who had been sitting so quiet and still, exploded from my side and took a running leap, teeth first, right in the middle of Jacinto Ocala's expansive face. Taz looked like a real Tasmanian Devil.

Chango screamed, "Get him off, get him off!"

Taz was shaking Chango's face like a portly rag doll, but only Chango was making any sound — the sound of agony. I called Taz, and surprisingly he let go, trotted back to my side, and sat down, like nothing had happened.

By now, the combination of the whacking of his forehead on my truck door, the whacking upside the head with my Smith & Wesson, and Taz's frontal assault on his fat façade caused Chango's face to look like a plate of *parisa. Parisa* is a Mexican delicacy composed of raw hamburger meat, onion, and a variety of spices. *Qué bueno!*

I didn't have to tell Chango to get up again. He struggled to his feet (or should I say foot, since he was still holding the wounded one).

"Up the stairs," I said pointing with my pistol.

Chango was about fifteen feet away from the stairs. He limped and hopped over to the bottom step with no additional prodding. I think he finally realized just how unkind both Taz and I could be.

"I can't make it up these stairs, man, my foot hurts too bad," Chango pleaded.

"Do the best you can," was my response.

Leaning on the guardrail, Chango hobbled up the stairs, pulling himself along with his hands.

When he got to the landing he looked down at me and asked, "Now what?"

"Jump," I said.

"From up here? You are a crazy motherfucker. That'll kill me!"

I carefully aimed my pistol and shot Jacinto in the left shoulder. He screeched.

"Jump," I repeated.

Chango clumsily climbed over the angle iron guardrail and more or less fell.

When Jacinto Ocala hit the hard red dirt, I could hear the bones in his feet, ankles and legs snapping. A sharp sound, like firecrackers going off in a swift chain reaction. As his more than ample body crumpled to the ground, he screamed in agony — and in fear.

I slowly walked from the bottom of the metal stairs to kneel before Jacinto. He was still screaming. I grabbed him by the front of his shirt and pushed his corpulent ass to his corpulent, pulverized knees. In the moonlight I caught a glint of white protruding from the thigh area of his jeans. It was his femur. His jeans were turning a dark red.

In a gentle voice I said, "Jacinto, shhh, be quiet. It will be okay. Real soon, I promise."

His screaming stopped. More from shock, I suspect, than my soothing voice.

Then I asked, "Jacinto Ocala, do you believe in God?" No answer. Chango was fading. I slapped him — hard. His eyes focused on me.

"Jacinto Ocala, do you believe in God?"

"Yes," he croaked.

"Then beg for His forgiveness," I whispered.

Nothing. I slapped him again. Like a Clapper appliance, he came on.

"Please forgive me, God. Oh, Jesus God. Please. Please. Please," he moaned.

"Now," I said, "I want you to beg for Angelita's forgiveness."

"Goddamnit, man, she's dead!" he wailed.

"It doesn't matter, Jacinto," I insisted, " you need to ask her forgiveness."

"Oh, Jesus, it hurts, it hurts, goddamn motherfucker. Please help me." He was now screaming.

"Shhh. Shhh. Jacinto Ocala, it's okay. I will help you, but first you have to ask Little Angel to forgive you."

Chango was losing consciousness. I couldn't let him go yet. I kicked his leg. Hard. It made a squishy sound and bent in places it shouldn't have.

He shrieked. "Shit, shit, fuck, ahhhhh, kill me, please, kill me."

Chango was not feeling well. The shrieking dissipated into an agonizing moan and then suddenly, for a few seconds, Chango became very quiet, very still. His eyes seemed to focus on something a few feet in front of him. A ghost, maybe?

Then he started, "*Angelita, por favor. Lo siento mucho, mi hija. Por favor, perdóname, perdóname, perdóname.*" Silence.

Again, I slapped him — hard.

"Jacinto Ocala," I said, "God does not forgive you. Angelita does not forgive you. And for whatever it's worth, I do not forgive you."

And with that, I put him down. With my Model 59 Smith and Wesson, I put the corpulent motherfucker out of his misery. And out of the misery of everyone else he had ever touched.

Because of his immense size, I would need help disposing of Chango's body. When I visited the old driller at Dawkins #6, I had noticed a backhoe. For all I knew, God put it there. Taz and I made the short drive from Buckholder #5, found the key in the backhoe and drove back to Jacinto Ocala's lifeless body. With Taz sitting next to me, I scooped him up in the front-end loader, and we made our way back to

Dawkins #6.

When a company drills a well, they construct a mud pit. This is where they dispose of the mud that is used in the drilling process. Drilling mud helps over-come the down hole pressure in the well to keep it from blowing out. The mud pits are large — in this case about twenty feet wide, forty feet long, and four or five feet deep (hard to tell since it was full of used drilling mud).

I dropped Chango in the thick, almost primordial, ooze. He sank like a boulder. The pit would be allowed to dry out. In a few weeks the mud trans-forms into something akin to concrete. The company then brings in a bulldozer and levels the banked earth around the pit, spreading it atop the dried mud. Then buffelgrass, and mesquite, and guajillo, and other brush country vegetation will reclaim the small scar upon the land. Jacinto Ocala will become fertilizer. Good job, Chango!

Taz and I returned to St. Charles Place. In a contest of who was showing the least amount of emotion, Taz and I would have tied for first place. I guess that's the way God wanted it. Who knows?

There were two hotels in Catarino. The first one I called, appropriately named Brush Country Inn, just so happened to have a Luther Axelrod registered there. "He's in number eleven. Would you like me to ring his room for you?"

"Oh no," I said, " I'll stop by and surprise him."

Another road trip to the big city. Taz and I drove to the Brush Country Inn. No vehicle in front of number eleven, so I dropped off a note. "Luther, bring

Dwayne and meet me at the Buckholder #5 well at 7:00 P.M. tonight. Just the two of you." Signed Jamey Maxwell.

The dog and I got to the Buckholder #5 about 6:00 P.M. It was getting dark. I parked the S-10 behind the tank battery so Luther and Dwayne would not know where I was coming from. The element of surprise, you know.

God and I had a plan for the two of them — and a peculiarly perverse plan it was. But when they drove up promptly at 7:00 P.M., the plan changed. They had someone with them. That someone was District Attorney Marisol Cortinas. *Qué lástima.*

God had forgotten to clue me in on Plan B, so from this point on, I would have to play it by ear, improvise, go with the flow, and all that jazz. God is not always a lot of fucking help.

Dwayne was driving. He stopped the Bronco and Luther stepped from the truck roughly pulling Mari with him. He had a gun pointed at her. Dwayne, at Luther's command, was reluctantly getting out on the driver's side. They were both surveying the scene as best they could, with only the truck's headlights penetrating the gloom of darkness.

"Come out Maxwell or I'll butcher your girlfriend," Luther shouted.

I was actually standing behind them, about thirty feet away, behind the mesquite tree that Angelita had been tied to. Luther and Dwayne had no clue where I was. I could have shot Luther in the back, easily, but if it didn't kill him instantly, Mari would be dead.

I heard Dwayne whispering, a little too loud,

"Luther, let's get the fuck out of here and forget this shit."

"Shut the fuck up, Doobie!" Luther replied.

I circled back around them. From behind the Buckholder #5, I walked out into the glare of the head-lights.

Mari shouted at me to run, but she knew I would-n't. I couldn't.

"So, just what is it you want to talk about, Maxwell?" Luther asked sardonically.

"Actually, I would like to describe in detail how I'm going to exterminate a couple of shit-eating rodents I know," I replied.

"Well, before you get to that, Dwayne and I would like to put on a little show for you," Luther lobbed back. "You see, we've been keeping an eye on you, Maxwell — you and your girlfriend here. It hurt my and Dwayne's feelings that she never invites us over to her cute little house. We're a little jealous, so we're gonna act out our feelings of frustration for you, so you will understand. A little show just for you."

"I doubt that it's anything I would be interested in."

"Oh, I think you'll definitely be interested. Excited even. I bet it'll even make you horny!" Luther added.

"By the way, Maxwell, you must've been the worst fucking investigator that ever worked for the fucking feds," Luther laughed, waiting for me bite on this line. But I didn't.

"You dumb fuck, we've been following you for a week and you didn't even fucking know it. Watched you with your little cunt here. You two lovebirds in a mall parking lot — how fucking sweet. Watched you with the crazy fucking bitches down the street from your little shithouse. Watched you talk to our old snaggle-toothed boss, Newton. Pretty much watched you do everything but take a shit and fuck the little lady here. Can't get it up?"

If this didn't get to me nothing would at this point. God's zombie/pseudo-archangel/wanna-be, Jamey Maxwell, was covered with a hard candy shell, but he wasn't soft and chocolaty on the inside. He was the penultimate avenging angel and maybe even God was afraid of him at this point.

Luther droned on, "A real tragedy it was. Yes, sir. It's the kind of tragedy that can drive a poor fucking guy insane. Make him rape and kill an innocent little girl; rape and murder a pretty little District Attorney; and then, when he can't take it anymore, kill his piti-ful fucking self. A real fucking tragedy."

Of course I knew what the game was as soon as I recognized Mari in the truck. He was planning to make me watch him and Dwayne torture and kill Mari before he killed me — it would look like a mur-der/suicide. But why would I want to stick around for something like that? I didn't. No, I didn't.

I certainly was not in a position to show a sign of weakness. That's exactly what Luther was looking for. He wanted his revenge to be sweet.

Luther's left arm was around Mari's fragile neck. With the snub-nosed pistol in his right hand he was obscenely rubbing Mari's breast through her gray pin-striped jacket and white silk blouse.

"You need to watch this, Maxwell? I'm gonna fuck

her — tear her up good. Then I'm gonna let Doobie have sloppy seconds, right Doobie?"

Dwayne replied nervously, "Let's just kill him Luther. Let's get it over with."

Luther laughed, "Relax Doobie. He ain't no problem. He's a big pussy. He ain't nothing and he ain't got nothing for you to be afraid of. So you just quit acting like a pussy yourself, Doobie, my man."

While Luther goaded, I was moving in barely noticeable increments, trying to position myself to use the Buckholder #5 gas well as a weapon. In the relative darkness, lit only by the headlights of Luther's Bronco, Luther and Dwayne had not yet snapped on my strategy.

Howard, the gauger, had shut the two-inch ball valve, located on the ground, some time ago to let the well build up pressure. I knew the well was shut in because I could not hear the gas flowing through the line.

Gas wells build up pressure at the wellhead and I knew from my experience as a gauger's helper that this gas well, the Buckholder #5, had about 1,800 psi shut-in pressure.

Howard, the gauger, had shut the Buckholder #5 in a couple of weeks earlier than usual for no apparent reason. But now the reason had become very apparent: God was pulling for the home team.

I needed to maneuver about three more feet to my right to get into an offensive position. Luther was still taunting me; spewing forth obscenities and torturing little Mari. Bantering with him to distract from my subtle drift toward the ball valve, I kept my eyes on

Mari. I was sending out strong psychic messages imploring her to be ready.

Then I started talking. "Luther, you and Dwayne don't have the balls to hurt a District Attorney. I doubt either one of you could even get a hard-on under these conditions or any other conditions for that matter. Except maybe by fondling each other," I said, pulling out all the stops.

At that point, Luther grabbed Mari by the hair and said, "Unzip his pants," pointing to Dwayne. She refused. Luther stuck the gun in her ear and said, "Unzip 'em, bitch! Now!" Mari unzipped Dwayne's pants.

"Pull his dick, out," Luther hissed. Again, Mari refused. Jerking her hair, Luther snapped Mari's head back and stuck the gun in her mouth.

"I'm gonna blow your fucking brains out right here! Pull it out, now! We're gonna show your boyfriend how Dwayne and I CAN get hard-ons. Pull Dwayne's dick out and make it hard or I'll kill you."

I could sense something changing in fearless Mari, something was going terribly wrong, she was disintegrating. Mari turned and looked at me. Even though Mari, Luther, and Dwayne were only about ten feet away, I could see just enough to read her eyes. The headlights were behind them, leaving a shadow on Mari's pretty face.

Fortunately, she could see me clearly and was receiving my transmissions, despite the fact the trauma was beginning to break her. But just when I needed her to, Mari acted. She seemed to be passing out. She let herself go limp. And Luther looked down just for an instant.

That's all I needed. I kicked hard at the thick metal handle on the ball valve. Instantly, 1,800 pounds of gas, condensate, and water vapor hit Luther, Dwayne, and Mari, knocking all three of them to the ground. The noise was deafening — like a freight train inside a tornado. Have I mentioned that the element of surprise can be a wonderful ally?

The blast had knocked the gun out of Luther's hand, and I screamed at Mari to grab it. And since she was a few feet closer, Mari beat Luther to the draw.

Quickly, Mari rose to a crouched position with her finger on the trigger, her left hand under the right, supporting the snub-nosed revolver, just as Arlen Buckner had trained her. Then she said to Luther Axelrod, "Don't move, motherfucker, or I'll blow your fucking head off." She would have.

Next, something happened that under less dismal and tragic circumstances would have been hilarious. Dwayne struggled to his feet, but was making no threatening moves out of fear of being blown away by what looked like a little girl who, on the way to church, in her best Sunday clothes, decided to jump in a mud puddle.

But that wasn't the funniest part. As Dwayne stood there stunned, looking like the drowned weasel that he was, Taz, again without a word, had soared into action. He took a flying leap, and, once more with flawless aim, landed, this time, on Dwayne's pasty face. Dwayne and the amazing acrobatic pooch went sprawling to the hard red dirt. The Tasmanian Devil had struck *otra vez*.

Diablo de Tasmania — 2
Los Diablos — 0

By this time, I was on top of Dwayne and Luther. Both of them were on the ground, one with a medium-sized canine attached to his face. Bearing down on them with my S&W 9mm, I screamed, "Get on your feet, assholes!" I was screaming not from the excitement and adrenaline, I was amazingly calm, but because the Buckholder #5 gas well was still roaring.

I called Taz off Dwayne's face. Again, I was surprised at how readily he obeyed. Luther and Dwayne rose unsteadily to their evil feet. I told them both to turn around. They, like Taz, were obedient.

"Mari, if they move, blow their fucking heads off," I said as I backed up the ten feet or so to the Buckholder #5. I shut the ball valve. The noise stopped.

Suddenly, the night was deathly quiet, the key word being deathly. Plan A — mine and God's original strategy — was back in vogue.

"Luther, you know that little show you and Dwayne wanted to put on, well you're gonna get your chance," I smiled.

"Mari, my truck's behind the tanks there. There's some rope in the bed. Go get it." And she did.

"Give the rope to Dwayne," I said. And she did.

"Now Dwayne, you see that mesquite tree there to your left. I bet you recognize it, don't you?"

"Take your asshole buddy, Luther Axelrod, and tie his arms around the trunk," I said.

"Don't do it, Dwayne. Don't do anything this prick

says," Luther hissed.

I cranked off a round that split the air between both their ears.

"Get moving," I suggested.

They both shuffled over to the large mesquite tree.

"Get on your knees, Luther," I demanded. He minded me. Luther was being a good boy.

"Put your arms around the tree. Dwayne, tie his hands." He minded me. Dwayne was also being a good boy.

I asked Mari to check the rope to see if it was secure. It was.

Now I started drifting inside my head. With God's assistance, I was letting my mind go blank and letting Him fill the void. From this point on, the words coming from my mouth would not be mine.

"Dwayne, pull Luther's pants off," I heard the voice speak. It sounded different, unearthly. Even Mari noticed. The rage in her eyes was replaced by disbelief. But it didn't really matter now. It was out of our hands.

"Don't do it Dwayne. I'll kill you, you son-of-bitch!" Luther screamed.

Luther, I think, had figured out what was going down. Dwayne was a little slower.

"He'll kill me if I don't, Luther," Dwayne said, and, of course, he was right.

"I swear I'll cut your fucking throat, Dwayne!" Luther was starting to panic.

I fired another shot across Dwayne's bow. "Do it now, Dwayne." And he did.

"The underwear too," I further instructed Mr.

DuBois.

"Dwayne, don't do it motherfucker!" was Luther's helpless response.

"I have to Luther, I have to," Dwayne whimpered. And he was right.

Mari had not said a word since the new and frightening voice had emerged from Jamey Maxwell's mouth. She was silently staring at me — for she had figured out the program.

"Okay, Dwayne, now take your pants off. Underwear too," came the strange intonations.

"Dwayne, please don't do this...don't make me hurt you, Dwayne," Luther was almost pleading. You could almost see the light bulb go on above Dwayne's pointed head. Now he understood. The look of indescribable fear and repugnance spread across his pockmarked face. But, as with Mari, there was also an air of resignation.

Dwayne didn't protest or even quibble. He simply, in a robot-like manner, stripped from the waist down. The freak show was getting freakier.

Luther was alternately threatening and pleading with Dwayne to stop, but I think I detected a trace of acquiescence in his evil soul. He had lost control of his world.

I pointed my gun at Dwayne's limp genitals and said, "Now, make it hard Dwayne."

"I can't. I...I...I just can't...please!" Wrong answer Dwayne. The bullet from the Model 59 ricocheted between Dwayne's legs.

Instantly, he started fondling himself — stroking rapidly back and forth. But the pressure and tension was too much for Dwayne. Nothing was happening.

Had there been even an inkling of sanity remaining inside Jamey Maxwell's head, what happened next would have been disturbing beyond belief. But madness was running amok that night on the Buckholder #5 lease. God had let loose the hounds of lunacy and vengeance and they were neither spayed nor neutered. There was no turning back.

Mari walked up to Dwayne DuBois and said flatly, "Don't worry, Dwayne. I'll make it hard for you." But it was no longer the Marisol Cortinas I knew speaking. And she did make it hard for him. Mari was acting out her role in this hellish drama, which was being directed from above, I suppose. And I stood there, watching, without emotion. I was a zombie. I was dispossessed.

"Now, Dwayne, get on your knees behind Luther," the disembodied voice spoke. "Do it now. Do it fast."

"I'm sorry Luther. . . they made me do this! I don't wanna do it. I . . . I . . . I'm sorry!" Dwayne sobbed.

Luther did not struggle and he could have. I would say I was surprised but that would be a lie. At this point in the Strangest Show on Earth, there were no more surprises.

Luther was silent for a second and then let out a piercing scream. The moans and the screams coalesced, as did Dwayne and Luther. It only lasted for a few seconds, but God's will had been done.

Dwayne, still crying, jumped up and began to run down the red dirt lease road. He only got a few yards before Taz caught up with him and silently brought him down.

Marisol and I looked at each other much as two cyborgs would — with vague recognition, but no feeling. I told her to switch guns with me. And she did.

By the time I arrived at Dwayne's side, Taz had pulled off. By now, Dwayne's nerves, I believe, had actually broken down — he was essentially incoherent. Babbling. As my old friend, Big Al, would say: "I think Dwayne is a Babylonian."

Dwayne was (I'm not sure inconsolable is the right word, but let's use it) inconsolable. He would mumble something unintelligible then he would scream, "God help me! God help me! God help me!" This from a man who had never used God's name in his life, except in vain, I'm quite sure. Dwayne was being sacrilegious. After a couple of minutes (I'm sure it seemed like hours to Dwayne), I grabbed him by his sweaty, greasy hair. I whispered in his sweaty, greasy ear, "Dwayne, listen to me. Shhh. Listen to me, Dwayne. God won't help you. No. No. No he won't. God won't save you, Dwayne. No. No, he will not save you. You know why? Because God doesn't like you, Dwayne."

I paused for a few seconds to let this sink in to Dwayne's corrupt skull. Then the punch line, "Dwayne," I said quietly, "Who do you think sent me?"

He was struck dumb with realization. Dwayne had an epiphany. At last, Dwayne had gotten the big picture. *Pintura grande.* From this point, all Dwayne could do was whimper. No words, just the sound prey animals make when felled by a predator, knowing that resistance is futile. When they know it's over.

Then I whispered into Dwayne's sweaty, greasy ear, "That's right Dwayne. Be quiet. Be still. It will all be over soon. But Dwayne, I want you to do me a favor. Okay? When you get where you're going, if you run into Leroy and Thomas Gohlke, give them my regards. Tell them I'll see them soon. And tell them I will have a special surprise for them. If they're not there yet, don't worry about it. You and I and Luther and Jacinto can greet them together, like one big happy damned family. So long, Dwayne."

With that, I put a hole in Dwayne's shit-filled skull with Luther's Charter Arms .38 Bulldog — just as I had promised. And I liked it — a lot.

By this time, Luther was silent. He knew the score. He was not going to beg and scream like his old buddy, Doobie. He was going to go out with a shred of dignity. And after what had just unfolded between Dwayne and him, a shred was all that was left. My question was this: Is dignity important to Satan? I doubt it. But Luther wasn't quite there yet.

Believe it or not, here's what I did. I untied him and after wiping for prints, I handed Luther his Charter Arms revolver. Mari stood behind me holding the 9mm on him.

Luther — naked from the waist down, sitting under the mesquite tree, his black greasy hair hanging in his face — smiled a malevolent smile and, with eyes glistening like something magnificent was happening, held the gun up to his temple, and blew his brains out.

An anonymous caller (from a payphone in Catarino) to the Losoya County Sheriff's dispatcher provided the following information: an apparent murder/suicide involving some kind of bizarre ritual between homosexual lovers had transpired on Buckholder #5 oil and gas lease, just north of Dos Cruces. The bodies were still there. The caller did not want to get involved.

Part III

Redemption, Resurrection, and Reparation

Chapter 1

Justice, at Last?

Anonymous tips were also transmitted by pay-phone (traced to a mall in San Antonio) to District Attorney Marisol Cortinas, Sheriff Arlen T. Buckner, and Jimmy Boyer, counsel for defendants Jamey Maxwell and Daniel Galván. The jist of the tips were identical: check DNA samples from Luther Axelrod and Dwayne DuBois with those found on Angelita Cavazos, then crosscheck with those obtained from Maxwell and Galván.

Of course the District Attorney's Office and the Sheriff refused to fork-up the moola for DNA testing, but Jimmy Boyer was more than happy to do the moola-forking. The results were a shock to D.A. Cortinas and Sheriff Buckner, but proved beyond a shadow of a doubt what Gentleman Jim Boyer had been telling the court all along: his clients were innocent and perpetrator or perpetrators, now known, had committed this heinous crime.

Judge Durán, after consulting with all parties, dropped the charges against Jamey Maxwell and Daniel Galván. Jimmy Boyer told the press his clients were relieved to be vindicated and had no hard feelings toward the justice system. Marisol Cortinas declined to comment to the press.

Sheriff Buckner expressed severe reservations about dismissing the cases against Maxwell and Galván, and was not totally convinced of their innocence. He would continue his investigations into the Cavazos murder and the apparent murder/suicide of Dwayne Dubois and Luther Axelrod. Sheriff Buckner was again afraid he was running out of reasons to exist. I know where he's coming from. Yes, I do.

Daniel Galván returned to Dos Cruces, Texas; to his family; but more importantly, to his beloved goats. For the first couple of days, I actually thought Daniel's grin would rip his face off. Daniel was one happy Dos Crucian.

Chapter 2

Into the Void

Marisol, as I had guessed would happen, was having trouble dealing with what she had done. A week after Daniel and I became free men, Mari called me. She asked if I would come over to her house after she got off work. She really needed to talk.

I arrived at her place at about 6:00 P.M. dressed in my nicest duds, which weren't all that nice: khaki shirt, jeans I had ironed myself, and my best and only sports coat. The one I had worn to visit Violet... the last time I saw her (although I had seen her crazy sister twice since then, but by herself, which was unheard of). My boots and my soul were scuffed and covered with the red-brown dust of Dos Cruces.

Mari met me at her front door dressed in her usual business suit and hesitantly invited me inside. Because of the hesitation, I was sadly convinced that she could no longer abide our relationship. Not now. Not anymore. Not after the atrocities that we, she and

I, had committed.

Marisol Cortinas couldn't handle the burning hatred that had surfaced that night on the Buckholder #5 lease. Or rather, she could not abide the results. Up until then, she had managed her anger — kept a lid on it nice and tight. But suddenly, due to no fault of her own, the bottled hate had exploded with catastrophic consequences to Luther, Dwayne, and herself.

I spent hours trying to convince her that what had happened was beyond her control. But control was everything to Mari. If she had lost her control, in her way of thinking, she had lost herself. Control was Marisol Cortinas' now totally useless defense mechanism. A little girl lost in a great big shit-filled world. I feared she would not be able to handle the consequences. Unfortunately, I was right.

The last thing we talked about before I left was this: Mari was considering turning herself in for the murders of Luther Axelrod and Dwayne Dubois. The only reason she hadn't done it yet was because of Jamey Maxwell.

My response was the following: (1) "Mari, you didn't kill those men;" and (2) "Mari, if you need to confess to what you have done or what you have seen, I understand."

For me, killing Jacinto Ocala, Dwayne Dubois, and Luther Axelrod was a contract murder for hire. The Big Guy ordered the hit and at some point in the future, payment would be made to Jamey Maxwell. In due time, as they say, in due time. But I was not sure in which currency compensation would be given. In lieu of cash or credit card, I would gladly accept oblivion.

Chapter 3

What Cost Redemption?

Come April, Marisol Cortinas resigned as District Attorney of Losoya County for reasons of health. I was not at all surprised.

Mari had called me several times since my last visit to her house. Like magma inside a volcano no longer dormant, guilt and grief were welling up inside the beautiful, damaged soul of Marisol Cortinas. And let me assure you, the damage to her soul was irreparable. God did not have to tell me this, the message was being transmitted directly over the phone line. SOS. Mayday. Meltdown. Of course, the depressing part was that Jamey Maxwell could do nothing but watch the tragedy unfold.

When I was still in high school, I attended an air show at the local naval station in Beckville. The Golden Knights, a United States Army skydiving team, performed. One of the soldiers got tangled in his parachute and the crowd could see the tragedy happening. Everyone watched in disbelief, horror, and helplessness. Then he hit the ground. This is how I felt each time I talked to Mari.

Foolish me, I even prayed to God on behalf of Marisol Cortinas. I asked Him to give her peace. I asked Him to provide some sort of comfort and solace. I asked Him to cut her some slack, Goddamnit. And in His own, inimitable way, I suppose He did.

Chapter 4

The Dead Resurrected

Begrudgingly at first, and recently with a peculiar reverence, I have come to love the brush country in general, and Dos Cruces in particular. The people, the animals, the plants, even inanimate objects. Superficially, the landscape is starkly forlorn, the trees and shrubs stunted and deformed, the creatures gaunt and unpretentious. But like much of life, it's a façade, a camouflage, a defense mechanism.

The mesquite and the cactus are constantly spreading their roots into new territories, opportunistically filling the void. Their mitigating shade and thorny countenance provide sanctuary for all manner of wild living things. Roadrunners and rodents, snakes and horned toads, ants and spiders, all thriving in symbiotic equilibrium while the harsh, seemingly dull, disguise convinces the rest of the world to pass by, never guessing the secret. It's as if a cosmic cop is saying, "Move along, nothing to see here."

Interestingly, after a preciously rare rain shower, the plants and animals let their guard down, at least for a few hours. Deer and javelina come out of hiding to cavort with their neighbors; the cenizo with its profuse lavender flowers blooms ephemerally; the mysterious tiny red velvet bugs, seen only after a rainfall, come out of their underground lairs to metamorphose. Then, as quickly as the revelry flourished, it is gone — just a sentient dream.

I began to feel better, not normal, not even close to normal, but better. Grief and guilt aside, Daniel's company was always a joy. And yes, Taz's too. But more than that, I was starting to look at things in a different light. With interest, I think. People, trees, animals,. . . Marisol Cortinas. It didn't last. God wouldn't let it.

Two days ago, my neighbor and favorite Dos Cruces detective, Ramón Falcón came over and asked if I would sit with *"el viejo que habla con los muertos,"* the old man who talks to the dead. Zaragosa, the old man, was dying. I guess he would be talking to himself soon.

Lucy, my dad's "girlfriend" (if you can call a 70+ year old woman a "girlfriend" — what the hell, let's call her that) had even told me the story of the old man relating a conversation he had with her long dead husband. Lucy was convinced the conversation had taken place. It sounded right to her. It didn't hurt, I think, that he had told Lucy her dead husband was at peace. That he was very happy in heaven and was looking forward to seeing her when the time came.

I asked Ramón, "What about a doctor?"

"The doctor won't come," he replied.

I didn't ask any more questions. I told Ramón I would sit with the old man — after all what else did I have to do?

The old man Zaragosa's place was worse than Dochler's. It was no more than 200 square feet, less than half of the roof was left, and the wood floor in what I guess was the kitchen had already collapsed from dry rot, age, and apathy. The old man was lying on a cot with a straw mattress. You could actually see the straw sticking out. The illusion was that of a horizontal scarecrow.

Next to the cot leaned a small, wooden table adorned with a statue of the Virgin of Guadalupe and a plastic cup of water. A straight-back wooden chair sat next to the little table. The only other piece of furniture in the shack was an ancient trunk at the end of the cot. On top of the trunk was a large ledger — the kind accountants use. The book was open and the two exposed pages were covered with an old person's handwriting. It was in Spanish.

Zaragosa was asleep or unconscious, I wasn't sure which, and I guess it didn't matter. The Dos Cruces story on old man Zaragosa was much like the one on old half-man Dochler. Zaragosa had worked on a large ranch somewhere around Dos Cruces. When he got too old to be of any value to the ranch owners, he moved to town. They say he had even ridden with Pancho Villa. Hey, not many folks still around to dispute that legend.

How long had he been living in Dos Cruces? "*Toda su vida,*" according to Ramón Falcón. Zaragosa was at least one hundred years old. His breathing was so shallow that every fifteen minutes or so I would place my hand on his bare, caved-in chest. His tired ancient heart was beating, but just barely.

Only a few weeks ago, you could still see the old man sitting out in his Dos Crucian, vegetation-free, back yard. He would sit on an old crate next to a large wooden spool — the kind the phone company cable comes on. The old man would be writing on something — the old ledger I suppose. Maybe his memoirs or transcription of his talks with the dearly departed.

Of course I had seen him myself many times during my three-year stint in Dos Cruces. But I had never once spoken to him. I don't think he even knew I existed. He didn't know me from Adam, or Eve, for that matter. And then after sitting with him for thirteen hours straight, he regained consciousness just long enough to tell me he was going to see my wife and my two beautiful daughters. This was too much for Jamey Maxwell... Jamey Maxwell go crazier... Jamey Maxwell want to die.

Ramón Falcón came back to relieve me. I went back to St. Charles Place to drink a few beers and to consider blowing my brains out with my trusty Smith and Wesson Model 59.

Chapter 5

The Meek Inherit Dos Cruces

The new couch was in place when Marisol Cortinas arrived, but just barely. Daniel and I had managed to squeeze it through the front door at a 53-degree angle, on the third try, about ten minutes earlier.

The blue and red plaid couch was the first piece of furniture, or the first piece of anything for that matter, that I had acquired since moving to Dos Cruces. Until now it hadn't really mattered. Jamey Maxwell's needs were simple. A simple man with a simple plan.

But for some reason, District Attorney Marisol Cortinas had changed the equation. I was acting like a high school kid on his first date. I kept telling myself to chill out, grow up, get real. She was just coming for supper. She was just being nice, just being sweet, just being beautiful and sexy — oh, shut up, Maxwell.

Nevertheless, when she finally arrived, I was as nervous as... well, as a high school kid on his first date. And I couldn't chill out, and I couldn't grow up, and I couldn't get real — didn't really want to.

When I answered the front door, I almost lost it completely. Marisol. . . Mari, I had only seen in professional attire. Dressed for success, prepared to do battle, kick some ass, uniform of the day. Even through the deadly fiasco with Luther and Dwayne, she had been a mess, but a stylishly dressed mess.

Now, here she was, Mari on my tiny front porch, in tight jeans; a midriff-baring, sleeveless, bright yellow knit top; peek-a-boo sandals; and ravishing black hair trailing down behind her shoulders.

Without warning, I felt a trickle down my left cheek, then my right. Tears. I had not cried when my father died. I had not cried when my wife and daughters died. I had not cried my entire adult life. And now, look at me. How embarrassing. I told her to come in and asked her to excuse me for a second.

But before I could turn, Mari grabbed my hand and with the delicate, slender fingers of her other hand, reached up and wiped my tears. She pulled me to her and wrapped her arms around me. Mari then said the two words that finished me off. She whispered, "It's okay." After a lifetime of grief, guilt, and selfish pride, I broke down, sobbing, just inside my front doorway.

"I'm so sorry, I'm so sorry." I kept repeating these words to her, to my Connie, my Julie, my Josie, and to God, I guess.

"Shhhh, it's okay," she said so softly.

After a couple of minutes, the tears began to recede and my sobs began to sound like hiccups. I felt drained, but somehow healthier. Like an exorcism, maybe.

Before I could regain my tenuous composure, Mari said, "Don't say anything. Don't apologize. Don't explain. Just make love to me now, on your somewhat tasteful new couch."

I laughed. She laughed.

Still holding on to each other, we shuffled over to the couch, giggling and sniffling (in my case). Then she reached up to unbutton my shirt and reflexively I stopped her. I don't know why. Mari looked up at me with a cute little smirk and began to de-shirt me.

Three years ago, I weighed one hundred ninety pounds. I hadn't been on a scale since then, but glancing down at my upper torso, I realized that I had dropped at least twenty pounds. I looked skinny. And white. The whitest guy in Dos Cruces, Texas, I thought to myself.

Without breaking eye contact, Mari began to unzip my jeans. She reached inside and touched me. For the last three years I had been, effectively, dead from the waist down. That no longer appeared to be the case. Mari, in a way, was a faith healer. She cured the lame and resurrected the dead. A regular Oral Roberts, my mind was about to say, except it never got passed the Oral. Mari had dropped to her knees.

There is a phenomenon that amputees sometimes experience after losing a limb, wherein they perceive an appendage that has ceased to exist. Phantom sensory perception or something. That's how it felt. The sensation seemed real, unreal, and surreal, all at the same time. So many years, so many chaotic emotions. But my mind was clear on one point: it did not want

District Attorney Marisol Cortinas to stop.

After a few minutes, I regained consciousness enough to realize that I was breathing heavily. I pulled little Mari to her feet, dropped to my knees and slipped her sandals off. Painted toenails and a tattooed anklet. Shit. I quickly unsealed her jeans and slid them down around her petite ankles.

I whispered urgently, "Sit down." And she did.

Hoarsely I said, "Lie back."

Mari had on white French-cut panties and I could see a resplendent, and magnetic, black triangle through them. It lured me forward. I began to kiss her through the gauzy material. I heard her gasp. My fingers raced my tongue to pull the diaphanous fabric aside. Then, like a hummingbird on its favorite flower, I tasted her. Delicious. My tongue probing deep inside, I couldn't get enough. Directly, my hungry lips found her tiny button that seemed to be straining to greet them. Oh so gently, I sucked and teased with my lips and tongue.

Mari put her hands gently in my hair, pushed up against my mouth, and said very softly, "Whatever you do, don't stop, Mister." And I didn't.

Afterwards, I could vaguely remember hearing screams — could've been me, could've been her, could've been both of us. Then I had a silly thought: who came first, the chick or the egghead. My mind works in mysteriously absurd ways. Suddenly, still lying on the couch, both of us pretty much defrocked, I had the creepy feeling we were being watched. I was right.

Slowly (for obvious reasons) removing my head

from Mari's breast, I looked to my left and was visu-
ally accosted by Taz — mine and Daniel's one-eyed
dog-like entity. He apparently had sneaked in when
Daniel and I were moving the couch. Taz was an
appropriate name, I think, since the Tasmanian Devil
was our favorite cartoon character. And Taz, the
pseudo-dog (and the cartoon character), seemed to be
a cross between a cartoon and a humanoid in that his
facial expressions conveyed anthropomorphic emotions.

Case in point: he, the dog-thing, was now looking
at me with a derisive sneer. He instantly reminded
me of a Bulgarian Olympic gymnastic judge. I truly
expected him to hold up a scoring card that said 2.9.
"Okay, so you think you could've done any better?" I
thought, but only to myself. I didn't know Mari well
enough yet to reveal my completely odd contempla-
tions.

When I turned back to look at Marisol, she was
gone. My beautiful Connie Lee had taken her place.
Half-dressed, she was looking at me, smiling, but her
eyes. . . her eyes. . . .

I awoke crying. No Connie Lee, no Marisol, no new
sofa. Only the one-eyed dog staring at me, this time
with pity. My S&W Model 59 was lying next to me on
the old beat up couch — the one nobody wanted.

Marisol Cortinas had died in a one vehicle "accident" in June. She had been on her way to Dos Cruces
at two o'clock in the morning. Sheriff Buckner was the
first on the scene and he did not take it well at all.
When Chief Deputy Gilbert Ramírez arrived, Arlen
Buckner was holding Mari in his arms, rocking her

back and forth. He was whispering something in her ear, but she was already dead. Deputy Ramírez tried to persuade Arlen to let her go, but he refused. He rode in the ambulance with Mari back to the Losoya County hospital.

At the hospital, Sheriff Buckner had to be sedated. I learned all of this from Ramón Falcón, my neighbor. His nephew is the Losoya County dispatcher who was on duty that night. His nephew got all of the intimate details from Deputy Ramírez and passed along the straight skinny to Uncle Ramón and probably five or ten thousand of his closest friends.

Autopsy reports on Marisol Cortinas showed no signs of alcohol or drug use. The pathology reports also turned out negative. Here's what God told me: Marisol Cortinas committed suicide because she could no longer endure the guilt and grief. So why the fuck am I still here? Why can't He just let me go? Why do I have to endure the guilt and grief? Why does He keep killing the ones that I love?

And for all of you out there, here's the answer: this was not about Los Diablos. This was all about Daniel Galván — no that's wrong. It's all about the meek inheriting the earth. But the problem is the meek aren't capable of handling this daunting task. There are not enough meek — or should I say there are too many unmeek.

So God will continue to torture those of us in between (I think you can figure out what happened to me on my ninth birthday, if you haven't already). He will drive us insane, to the point where we will help thin out the herd of earth-dwelling belligerents. The assholes, the wrongdoers, the evil ones. It truly is a dirty rotten job and I didn't volunteer.

And why did God wait so long to take care of this little problem, you ask? How could He let this delicate balance of power shift from the good guys to the bad guys? Why now, after millions of years and billions of people on this trivial, insignificant orb on the outskirts of His universe? (I must talk faster now. Sheriff Arlen Buckner just drove up in front of St. Charles Place...getting out of his white, covered with red-brown dust, patrol car...strange smile on face.) Why did God not stop it before it got out of hand?

Here's why: because it took that long for Him to get to the point where He could no longer endure His own guilt and grief. You see, forty-one years ago, I made a deal with a God who was no longer in His right mind. Yes, boys and girls, God, your God, the One you call Lord, Jehovah, Allah, Buddha, Vishnu, or by other appellations. The One you get down on your knees and pray to at night or anytime you really need or want something. The One you talk to in church, or mosque, or synagogue, on Sunday, or Saturday, or Wednesday. The One who takes your loved ones away from you without explanation or justification. The One you look to for mercy...is, as I am, completely and hopelessly insane.

The End

A preview of the first three chapters of

The Vinegaroon Murders

VOLUME TWO OF THE DOS CRUCES TRILOGY

by

James A. Mangum

Chapter 1

The Santero

Her eyes half-closed, her lips slightly parted, the look of pure ecstasy. How long has it been? How long has he worked for this? How many times has he run his hands up and down her flawlessly smooth body? That look of rapture. So perfect, so serene, so final — *La Virgen de Guadalupe*. The carving is finished at last.

Chapter 2

The Sheepherder

Manuelito smells death. *Muerte*. Although he is only seventeen, it is a smell that has become all too familiar in his life. And death has come to him in many forms: coyotes, an occasional golden eagle, on rare occasions, wild hogs, but more often than not, dogs. Packs of semi-wild dogs. They are a sheepherder's worst enemy. In Manuelito's case, they have killed hundreds of his sheep over the last eight years. Dawn is breaking and the smell of death is in the air. But today it is different. And as yet unseen. It is May 15.

By nine o'clock, with the West Texas heat already building, Manuelito discovers the two bodies. A man and a woman amongst the rocks. They are covered with vinegaroons. Manuelito calls the vinegaroons *alacranes del diablo*. Devil scorpions. Although he has covered the forty square mile ranch thousands of times over the last eight years, he has seen a vinegaroon only two or three times. And only at night. Now he sees dozens of them scurrying over the dead couple, pinchers gnashing and whiptails thrashing. Here, in the light of day, they are frantically searching for something. Souls perhaps?

Manuelito mumbles, "*Dios sabe lo que hace,*" makes the sign of the cross and starts to cry.

Chapter 3

The Seraph

Jamey Maxwell is dreaming of angels. Seraphim. Cherubim. Thrones and Dominions. And, of course, the Fallen Ones. He recognizes almost every face. His sweet Josie... Julie, so beautiful... Connie Lee, but... where are her eyes? Luther and Dwayne. No Chango though. Marisol smiles at him, but she's been crying. He wants to tell her it will be okay, but he is unable to speak. He awakes, choking.

The dreams, the nightmares, come every night now, after a year of sweet respite. He suspects working with the Santero is not helping things. This is irrelevant, of course, because God chooses to project these images into Jamey's dreams. You humans would call it brainwashing. And what Jamey is seeing is not actually Seraphim, Cherubim, etc. He could not survive that experience. He is seeing a diluted, sanitized, humanized version of angels... something he can live to tell about, if he chooses to. I doubt that he will.

Jamey no longer speaks of his conversations with God or his visions. He wants to appear somewhat normal. He wants to live in the real world again. Fat chance.

How do I know all of this? Well, let's just say that I am one of God's messengers. A Watcher. An angel if you will. What theologians, especially Jewish theologians, would call a Seraph. But let me get this straight up front. Ancient Hebrew prophets, particularly Enoch, defined the nine choirs of the heavenly hierarchy and they got it surprisingly accurate with one major and a few minor exceptions. Seraphim are not the highest order of angel. Oh no. Quite the opposite in fact. Here is the true order (at least as far as humans can understand it), from highest to lowest: Cherubim, Thrones, Dominions, Powers, Virtues, Principalities, Archangels, Angels, Seraphim. There you are. I'm at the bottom of the celestial food chain. For human comparison's sake, let's just say that my name is Shyanne and I live in a trailer park in Del Rio, Texas. And let's just say I work as a barmaid at the Come On Inn, Highway 90 west, on the outskirts of Del Rio. Just trying to give you something to wrap your mind around.

A couple of other things before we get on with this story: guardian angels exist, but not in the way humans imagine. You would not want to see them. Visualize every monster under the bed or in the closet when you were a child, rolled into one and on steroids, acid, and crack cocaine. They are not really angels. They are a separate species. This is why they are not included in the nine choirs which I mentioned. What apes are to humans, guardian angels are to angels. And they are often, but not always, on the same side as the good guys. They are not rational beings. The universe would be better off without them, but what can I say. It's God's will. Don't bother trying to understand it.

And speaking of God's will, there is only one mortal sin in God's eyes and it's not included in the Ten Commandments, Bible, Koran, Torah, or other sacred writings. It's the one thing most of mankind has never gotten, to mankind's eternal shame and punishment. The one mortal sin, the one that God never forgives, is presumptuousness. Specifically, presuming to know God's will. Because He doesn't always know it Himself. God does not like to be second-guessed. So, a little hint before we continue with this tale: if you have a bumper sticker on your vehicle that reads, "In Case of Rapture, This Car Will Be Unmanned," I would invest, ASAP, in a razor blade and remove said bumper sticker. And, oh yes, if you actually believe the bumper sticker, I would invest, ASAP, in a frontal lobotomy. Never forget this point. Now to the story.

About the Author

James A. Mangum was born and raised in South Texas. He has lived and worked throughout the United States for the federal government as a Sky Marshal and Special Agent with the U.S. Treasury Department, a Federal Game Warden, an Investigator with the Office of Federal Investigations, and a Civil Rights Manager. He has been a co-owner of an oil and gas business and has most recently moved to Shiner, Texas, "the cleanest little city in Texas," where he now works as a folk artist, rescuer of wayward homes, and a teller of tales.